THE CASE OF THE FEAR MAKERS

LOHM find themselves involved in the affairs of one of the oldest of the private distillers' companies. New wine in old bottles seems to follow the trend of the adage as disaster follows disaster. It is almost impossible to say whether a murder was a murder, or what happened to the body. The mystery is in the hands of John Marsh and his two lady partners, who are very nearly split for ever by some sort of spectre. But can spectres shoot and kill? Nothing is impossible when a secret recipe is worth a fortune.

Books by John Newton Chance in the Linford Mystery Library:

SCREAMING FOG
THE DEATH WATCH LADIES
TRIANGLE OF FEAR
THE MAN WITH TWO HEADS
THE GUILTY WITNESSES
THE DEAD TALE-TELLERS
THE MURDER MAKERS
DEAD MEN'S SHOES
THE SMILING CADAVER
MADMAN'S WILL
LOOKING FOR SAMSON
THE MONSTROUS REGIMENT
THE CAT WATCHERS
THE CANTERBURY KILLGRIMS
A BAD DREAM OF DEATH
THE HALLOWEEN MURDERS
TERROR TRAIN
THE SHADOW OF THE KILLER
A PLACE CALLED SKULL
DEATH UNDER DESOLATE
END OF AN IRON MAN
DEATH OF THE WILD BIRD
RETURN TO DEATH ALLEY
THE MAYHEM MADCHEN
THE DEATH IMPORTER
THE THUG EXECUTIVE
A WREATH OF BONES

JOHN NEWTON CHANCE

THE CASE OF THE FEAR MAKERS

Complete and Unabridged

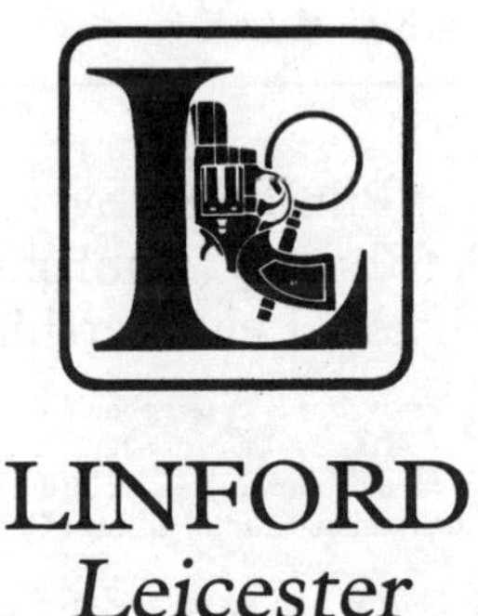

LINFORD
Leicester

First pu[illegible] in 1967 by
Robert Hale Limited
London

First Linford Edition
published 2004
by arrangement with
Robert Hale Limited
London

British Library CIP Data

Chance, John Newton, *1911 – 1983*
The case of the fear makers.
—Large print ed.—
Linford mystery library
1. Detective and mystery stories
2. Large type books
I. Title
823.9′14 [F]

ISBN 1–84395–422–2

Published by
F. A. Thorpe (Publishing)
Anstey, Leicestershire

Set by Words & Graphics Ltd.
Anstey, Leicestershire
Printed and bound in Great Britain by
T. J. International Ltd., Padstow, Cornwall

This book is printed on acid-free paper

1

The gymnasium of the LOHM Company thudded and panted to the ragged rhythm of the tired executives' swing. John Marsh's voice, clear and almost threatening, made the count; in-out, up-down, one-two. Sixteen tired executives in vest and shorts laid on their backs and raised their tired knees up to their overstrained bellies, gasping from the sudden pressure. Some, in trim, exercised smoothly, trying hard, almost grimly. Each man came three evenings a week on his way home and began to feel at last the pleasures of fitness.

That is, for a short time. Half-way through the exercise session the warm feeling of well-being would come on them. This would fairly glow under the hot and cold showers to follow. Their clothes would feel new and smooth and cool. As soon as they had them on and admired their new selves in the dressing-room mirror, they marched out into the lush bar and drank away all the new-found benefits. After all, they were mostly executives.

John Marsh at the founding of LOHM had used a gimmick from a famous London restaurant, where, once a man was segregated from his wife by the entrance saying, 'Gentlemen's Cloak Room', he turned the corner and found a bar laying in wait for him before the lavatorial equipment showed.

'The wives will encourage the men to exercise and keep fit and all the rest of it,' John Marsh had said, 'but the men won't stay if there isn't a pub or a club next door or a bar indoors.'

So they had a bar and a lanky, impudent barmaid by the name of Sheila, who, without any figure at all — some said it was like a pair of knitting needles tied in the middle — made every man feel male and pleased and full of wicked intentions.

The bar opened only in the evenings, when the gym classes were held. During the day, Sheila modelled under the nick-name of Scrimpy.

While the gym still thudded to the ragged rhythms of the panting men, Mary Adur, checking stock in the bar, came up behind Sheila who did not look round but lit a cigarette.

'Better lay in tremendous stocks of Royal G., cherub,' Sheila said.

'Why?' Mary said.

'Why the shaggy man, lion-like, that is, new member is the owner of Royal G. Didn't you know?'

'Mannfred?' Mary said, surprised. 'Funny. I didn't connect. How did you know?'

'Look, precious,' Sheila said. She held up a gilt bottle of liqueur and pointed out the coloured Regency head of a man encircled in gold on the label. 'It looks like him.' ' 'Richard Mannfred, friend of the Prince',' Mary read. ' 'For whom he made this rich, unmatched liqueur in the last years of George the III's reign'.'

'It looks dead like him,' repeated Sheila. 'That clued me.'

'Except his hair hangs over his eyes,' said Mary. 'That is when he is doing toe-touching. I wonder how he does it. I don't think he's seen his toes for years.'

'Here they come,' Sheila said. 'Limber up, matey.'

They heard the cheerful voices of the done-goods in the passage, crowding into the changing-room. Mary went out and into the gym. It was empty. Jane Shore, fourth member of LOHM, was showing judo holds to a keen businessman who was sweating shinily in his determination to get the hang of it.

Mary drew out again and went into the office across the passage. She put her order book on top of a filing cabinet, then slid out a drawer and referred to Mannfred's details which John Marsh had taken on his joining the previous day.

His measurements were prodigious, his weight formidable, his age, forty-three, expected, but it was noted that he had three scars on his ponderable belly, sword wounds.

'Sword wounds!' Mary said.

John Marsh came in, a towel round his neck, his slacks and jersey impeccably white. He was big, tall and plump like a wrestler.

'What's this, Mannfred? Sword wounds?' Mary asked.

'Unusual,' said John. 'So is Mannfred. He is to have a brief clash of épées with Jane in two minutes, just to see if he has the knack still. Apparently he hasn't fenced for some years.'

'But this is sword wounds, not foil pricks.'

The judo aspirant walked by, waddling a little, outside the open door. He smiled in before he pushed open the changing-room door and vanished behind its light flashing smoothness.

'Let's see how he shapes,' John said, turning back to the door. 'He has much weight but he moves fast. Some character.'

'He owns the liqueur firm,' Mary said, following.

'Yes. I looked him up. It's been in the family getting on for a couple of centuries. Still a family concern, too, though goodness knows how many of the top distillers have been trying to grab it these last few take-over decades.'

They went to the doors of the gym. Jane and Mannfred were taking guard. He looked too fat to stand a chance, like one of those Chinese laughing gods.

The impression was momentary. From the moment of the action his speed was fantastic. His wrist and arm moved with incredible agility, his foil clashed and darted like a snake's tongue. Jane gave ground. Fully on the defensive against his speed and accuracy, she had no time for attack at all. The play lasted a minute, then Mannfred threw his sword and free hand up and laughed. 'Some things last,' he said, and chuckled.

'They certainly do!' Jane said, pulling her mask off and shaking her fair hair free. 'Where did you learn?'

'Away at school,' he said. 'We used to play at it, with no buttons. If you lost, you were stuck, like a pig, and some used to scream too, like a pig.' He chuckled again, put his things down and took up a big, loose sweater. 'Miss Shore, I have a confession to make. My purpose here is a double one.'

They began to walk towards the exit.

'Double in what sense?'

'Double defensively,' he said. 'Ah, here is Mr. Marsh. Miss Adur, good evening. You heard what I was saying?'

'I caught a double,' Marsh said.

'Perhaps we can use your office,' Mannfred said.

They went into the office and sat down. Mannfred accepted a cigar, then reached forward to a tape recorder on the desk and set it going. Then he smiled and sat back, looked first at Mary, then at Jane, his eyes twinkling, then to John Marsh and the twinkle stopped.

'Your side operations, Mr. Marsh, proceed under the title of Extra Security Protection — Industry. Industrial counter-spies.' He chuckled. 'You are successful, or have been, so far. Here is another opportunity for you to succeed.'

He watched the tape a moment.

'So this is defence of the person, defence of the property,' Jane said.

'I hope so,' Mannfred said. 'My business was founded by a great-great-grandfather, friend of Prince George, whose palate was so jaded with riches he was desperately eager for new tastes, new flavours. My ancestor produced Royal G for him. The naming is obvious. It turned out that, good as it was for the Prince, it was better for customers who really had some taste left. For a hundred and seventy years it has flourished and so has my family. In the last generation we have expanded to the limit of what we can manage and our world distribution is of the greatest value. Any further expansion, however, would mean deterioration in the product. I won't have that.'

He smoked a while, thinking.

'Several large distillers and other drink firms have been after us for years. Very generous offers. Over generous, some. But anything to get control of the business and the name, then let the product gradually deteriorate with modern production methods, and let profits accrue in proportion.'

'You've refused all such offers,' Marsh said.

'I shall continue to refuse. Being a private family concern there is no legal way to force our selling ourselves to anyone. My financial position, and that of the business is such that I don't have to.'

'You seem reasonably secure,' Marsh said, watchfully.

'Until recently,' Mannfred said. 'We have a nucleus of old workpeople who have been with us for years. We try to induce their sons to come in with us, and we pay enough to make them come. That way, we seemed, as you say, reasonably secure. Recently, however, there have been signs of some kind of interference at our distillery at Lake Trance. We can't place it, but it is definitely taking place. Some of my employees are nervous, and this is a very bad thing for an old established family business. It begins to destroy confidence.'

'The recipe for Royal G,' said Marsh. 'This is a secret still?'

'Oh yes. The original paper, in John Mannfred's hand, is still in my possession, though it is an insurance against accident more than anything else. It is the tradition that the son learns the recipe from his father, and is passed to no one but his eldest son. It all sounds very melodramatic in these days, but nevertheless, it is the heart of our business. Without it, it must die.'

'What kind of interference?' Mary asked.

'Various incidents, indirectly carried out which suggest to me a deliberate campaign of intimidation. But not, you understand, definite enough for me to take any police action about it. I have the idea that it will increase, and that by the time it does I shall be hogtied by trouble with my workpeople and be unable to take police action.'

'It's becoming a popular way of dealing with obdurate owners of businesses,' Marsh said. 'I've heard of one or two cases which seem to suggest someone has set up an organisation selling this form of — what would you call it? — infiltration by fear.'

'It's a development of the protection racket,' Jane Shore said. 'But here force is kept well in the background. The attack, to start with, is more psychological.'

Mannfred sat back and smoked, his eyes narrowed.

'I see. So my suspicions of interference were correct.'

'It's quite likely,' Marsh said. 'Have there been any offers recently?'

'Not very recently. The last was a firm of Virginian Bourbon blenders who threw up dollars like confetti. That was finally rejected a month back. I don't suspect them. I don't suspect any of the big booze buccaneers. I have the feeling this is someone new, using something new.'

'You could find out who is behind it by putting out a whisper you might sell,' said Mary.

'I am a superstitious man,' said Mannfred, the twinkle back in his eyes. 'I don't use lies that could become truth. In fact, I'm so superstitious I might persuade myself into making it truth.'

'The distillery is in your own grounds at Trance?' Marsh said.

'How far is it?' Jane asked. 'From here?'

'Seventeen, about,' said Mannfred. 'LOHM is very handy for me.' He smacked his fat belly and laughed. 'Do me good to walk, perhaps.'

'You don't suspect any firm or person?' Mary asked.

'No. There's nothing direct. Like suspecting a ghost. Nothing's stolen. Nobody's hurt. It's a feeling as if the foundations have suddenly dissolved and there's nothing but ten thousand feet of air underneath.'

'We sometimes find,' said Jane, 'that if it's known who we are when we move in on a firm, things stop happening.'

'That's where the LOHM cover pays dividends,' said Mannfred, his eyes twinkling again. 'Yes. I think it could be in my case. So what do we do?'

'New advertising matter for the States?' Marsh suggested.

'We use Space Limited for our work,' Mannfred said.

'The interferers would know that, if they've got real gen on you,' said Jane. 'Then what?'

'Fit me up a gym,' said Mannfred, pointing at Jane with his cigar. 'That would cover us. Teach me at home. Remeditive exercise, fencing practice.

There is a ballroom that gets used once in a blue moon. Fine pine floor. Just the thing. I'm taking fitness seriously at last. Don't worry. I mean to go through with it — the fitness part. If you have to fight, it's best if every part of you is in good working order. That's it.'

'And when would the lessons be?' Jane asked. 'We have our classes here.'

'We can arrange that. I just want you to be around the damn place, armed with a good excuse for any-time appearances. Will you undertake?'

'Give us details,' Marsh said. 'Then we'll see.'

Mannfred put his cigar down and unloaded. He retained his essential secrets, but he unfolded the picture of his house by the lake where his great-great-grandfather had first learned to brew gold.

* * *

Trance was a Queen Anne mansion. It stood among trees on a slight hill looking down over the lake, a quarter mile away.

The lake shore was lined with firs on the house side, and on the southward-running shore the shape of the distillery stood amongst the trees, nestling there, a place of wood and brown brick, big mansard roof like a barn, three storeys high, a wood landing stage running out from it into the mirror of the lake.

Far up the lake a canal drove out, connecting with the old canal system. Barrels of Royal G were still taken out by barge across the lake, into the canal through the lock and along through the narrow waterway into the Wey, then into the Thames. Cases of the precious stuff were loaded on to lorries almost as long as the barges, and driven away through the pine woods on to the Camberley road, thence to every point of the compass. The workpeople came in along that road through the pines on cycles and in cars, and in the bus provided.

'The difficulty,' said Mannfred, 'is to find you an excuse to go down there.' He pointed to the old brown building on the lake shore.

They stood at the window of his office

in the mansion, looking down over the lake. John Marsh surveyed the beauty of the lake and the forest around it.

'There is someone there at night?'

'Often we work at night. Her Majesty's Customs man has to go short of his bed.' Mannfred laughed.

'Where does he come from?'

'Weybridge. Seven miles up the canal.' Mannfred pointed along the lake. 'He takes his toll of every fluid ounce we make.'

'Where does the water come from? For manufacturing?'

'Springs up in the wood,' Mannfred pointed again to the trees behind the distillery. 'That's part of our secret, the excellent water there. It's one of the things I am nervous about. The easiest thing to interfere with.'

'There hasn't been any sign of interference at the springs?'

'No, but as I say, it would be easy.'

'The spirit that you use is distilled down there?'

'Yes, it is a true distillery.' Mannfred turned to a table littered with invoices, letters, customs notices, chits and travellers' cards. It was a true old family business run in a true old family way. Untidily.

'Hasn't anyone told you you could make money with decent filing and machinery?' Marsh said, grinning.

'We could make more Royal G with machinery, but it wouldn't have the bouquet, nor the goodness,' Mannfred said and poured two glasses of the liqueur. 'Do try this.'

'I know it,' said Marsh. 'And I'm willing to try almost any time.' He drank appreciatively. It rolled smooth and honeylike on his tongue, rich and quiet, cool and strong. 'It makes you want to drink it. There's something sensual about it.'

'The greedier it makes you, the better we like it. Now, I want you to meet my wife, Maureen.'

He led the way out of the big office room into a smaller one and then stopped short. Marsh also stopped short just behind him.

A glorious red-headed woman of

around thirty was standing perfectly naked on a small weighing machine in the middle of the room.

'What on earth are you doing?' Mannfred said, tempering his startled tone with firm control.

'Weighing,' said Maureen, looking up. 'What do you think?' She looked at Marsh with eyes of purest green and smiled. 'Hallo,' she said. 'Who are you?'

Mannfred went across and took a silk dressing-gown from the back of a chair. Maureen went towards Marsh, a delighted smile on her beautiful face. Mannfred followed her quickly, as if trying to catch a butterfly in a net.

'Are you the physical man?' said Maureen, stopping and eyeing Marsh's shoulders and chest and general build.

Mannfred thrust the gown on to her shoulders. She just let it hang there.

'Will you teach me, too?' she said. 'I'm getting a spare tyre, for sure. Look.'

'Mr. Marsh — ' said Mannfred in sharp tones, ' — is here to see what fittings we shall want — Do do that gown up, Maureen darling! I'm sure Mr. Marsh finds it quite warm enough in here.'

She laughed and loosely slipped the silk tie together in a knot in the middle. Her eyes were on Marsh's, his on hers. A smile lit both their glances. It was instant desire. Marsh had felt it before, but couldn't remember it quite so suddenly as this.

'Now you show us what you're going to do,' Maureen said, in a soft, Irish accent. 'Me husband is determined to be as slim as a rake, which I don't like, but he says he will want to be in the fashion, which I think looks underfed, but there, he is a wilful man.'

Marsh couldn't see Mannfred slim. He wasn't the build.

Angry, Mannfred crossed the room and went through another door which led into a vast room with a minstrels' gallery, and windows looking out over a terrace and the lake. There were big chairs and settees lined up around the walls, almost lost in the vast place and looking like forlorn ghosts under the white dust sheets.

'This,' said Mannfred.

John Marsh looked round. He could

feel the green eyes smiling at him, feel the soft transmission of desire though he had his back to her.

'What do you look up there for, then?' she said, coming to his side and staring up into the high, painted ceiling, as he did.

'Seeing where we can sling the rings,' Marsh said.

'Nobody told me your name. Richard forgets.'

Marsh told her.

'We all have first names,' said Maureen. 'John, where will you put the rings? They have to be strong.' She laughed.

Marsh glanced at Mannfred but the distiller had quite recovered his good humour and laughed with his wife at the reference to his weight.

A middle-aged woman came in, a big, busty, commanding person yet with a half-smile on her face.

'Telephone, Mr. Richard,' she said.

'Thank you, Clarice. Excuse me.' He went out with her.

Maureen looked at John Marsh. He felt the tingle of electricity in her presence.

She was what Mary called a hot line.

'Richard's been worried about spies,' she said. 'Do you know spies? Why should they want to come here, then? For sure ye can buy the stuff anywhere for five pounds. Why do you want to spy? Do you think he is imagining little people?'

'I don't know,' John Marsh said. 'Lots of funny things go on these days. Perhaps they're spying on the gymnasium.'

'Well, that is a good idea, isn't it? My mother was very hard working and strong and healthy and had seven daughters, all beautiful like me.' She ended with charming frankness and laughed. Then she became grave and went close to him. 'You don't think Richard is — involved?' She looked anxious then. 'He travels so much. All sorts of people. He goes to foreign places and sells — there might be something attached sometimes.'

It occurred to Marsh that she was pumping him for something about Mannfred she didn't know. He found it hard to resist the wide, beautiful, anxious eyes.

'I don't know,' he said. 'Your husband is just a client of ours. We know nothing about him, except who he is. I don't imagine he needs to get mixed up with anything.'

'I mean, somebody might have followed him back here,' she said urgently.

'Why?' Marsh said. 'Have you seen anything? I mean, it's a funny kind of thing for a wife to say, unless there's some very good reason.'

'I think — ' She broke off and looked quickly, almost in alarm, towards the door Mannfred had gone out of. 'I think I have been followed.'

'That can't be anything new,' he said, smiling.

She smiled back. She responded to warmth like a mirror to the sun.

'This,' she said, 'is not like that. Nothing pleasant. Nothing flattering. Just — horrible. Followed but never anyone showing. That is like being watched.'

Another possibility occurred: that Mannfred might be having his wife watched. There could be reasons for that. He had seen one, standing on the scales. He had never seen quite such a lack of inhibitions. She had been delighted to have him see her nude, no matter that she had never seen him in her life before.

'It's creepy,' she said. 'Ye know, one time at home we had the banshees. Nobody believes in them, they say. It's when you feel them it's worst. Then you do believe them. They don't always scream, but they creep about round the house outside, and ye can see them peering in — that is, ye don't see them quite, but ye *know* — '

The more excited she became the broader came the brogue. It showed a sincerity that nothing else could have done. Marsh began to understand Maureen. She was just a damn kid at heart. She had still the terrors of the bog and the leprechauns.

'Where did you meet Richard?' he said.

'At home. He came fishin' for salmon. All by himself, bless him. To think, he said. I didn't let him think much. I fell in love like mad with him without knowin' in hell who he was. I even felt a bit sorry I'd been such a whore. I would have liked him to be the first. I wish to God I never told him that, too.'

She walked a little way off then turned and her sadness faded and became a smile. Her volatility was remarkable.

Marsh wondered how much of a secret she would keep back under pressure of some acute, but passing emotion. Or even the suggestion of espionage fairies at the bottom of this vast garden.

Mannfred came back with Mary Adur.

'Your secretary has arrived, Mr. Marsh,' Mannfred said, and glanced at Maureen.

A brief flash of anger passed across Maureen's face, and fire came into her eyes. Then she turned away and smiled at Mary, eyes grown cold and critical. Mary smiled back. She had a notebook.

'What apparatus have we available at the moment, Mary?' Marsh asked.

Mary read out some stuff. The Irishwoman wandered away and looked out of the window down to the lake. Mannfred walked up and down the huge room, slowly, as if measuring it by eye.

There was a sudden atmosphere of waiting, of tension as the shadow of the dark green trees grew longer on the west side of the water.

Mary read out a list of things. Marsh interrupted at certain points. Now and again he looked at a pocket watch as if anxious over the time.

Maureen lost patience, excused herself with a brief fiery glance at Marsh, and went. John opened one of the tall window doors, looked out, then consulted his watch again.

Once more the middle-aged secretary came in and once more Mannfred went out with her. Mary went over to John and he looked at the watch a final time.

'Is it bugged, this room?' she asked quietly.

'It was,' he said. 'The old kicker was leaning over to bust out of the case just now. Now there's no reaction at all.'

'Switched off?'

'No. I think the good lady must have had a bug in her pocket.'

'The secretary?'

'No. The lady.'

'She didn't look as if she had much in the way of pockets,' Mary said with a cold inflexion in her voice. 'That gown had none, and there wasn't anything else, was there? Bare feet even.'

'There was nothing else,' John said.

He looked at the radio transmission indicator for the last time. The kicker, set where the second hand should have been, was still. There was no radio transmission taking place anywhere near them now.

Mannfred came back.

'If you've decided,' he said, 'I'd like to take you round the lake — on the road, that is. It is really very beautiful by evening. The colours in the water are quite incredible.'

They went out and into an open Land-Rover standing by the door with John's, Mary's Imp and a couple of other cars. No one was about.

As he got into the open vehicle, John looked round. There was a girl standing in the window of a room. He thought it was the wife, but then saw she was a smaller, fairer girl altogether. As he saw her, she turned away and vanished into the darkening room.

Richard drove away from the house.

'I had a message from the Vat,' he said

tersely. 'It seems the watchmen have noticed prowlers near the loading yard within the last half hour.'

'Have they noticed it before?'

'On two occasions. They make a report every morning if anything happened during the night. Twice recently there have been mentions of shadowy figures outside. The first time it said, 'Poachers', which we do get, for sure.' He laughed. 'The second time it said, 'Suspicious persons'. Now they've called me on the phone to go down and see.'

'Have they said what the difference was in the case of the behaviour on each occasion?' John asked.

'No. They didn't say anything of that.'

'Gave no reason why the suspects should be first harmless poachers, then suspicious characters, now something that justifies an alarm?'

'Not that I know of.'

'Could be just tensions growing up with the repetition,' Mary said.

'That could be right,' Mannfred said. 'As I told you, it is a series of small unexplained things which have started this rot in people's confidence. Things that just shouldn't be there. Things that won't be explained.'

They drove on down the narrow road with the tall pines towering above them on either side. On the right the blue evening water of the lake showed between the hundreds of straight tree trunks.

'What staff do you have in the house?' John asked.

'We run eight by day, and keep a couple of girls by night because of international business. People will ring from San Francisco forgetting what time it is here, so we cover that with a night watch in the office.'

'Clarice?'

'Clarice stays any old time. She is a spinster with no one and I think is lonely at home, so she stays countless hours. Quite the old-fashioned family business retainer.'

He laughed.

The track swung round and joined a wider road, then both ran into the yard of the Vat. It towered up against the evening sky, a gaunt giant of brown, black-streaked boarding and brown brick fill-ins. The windows were wood and small-paned, hardly anywhere square, but twisted with the years. It had a warmth, a character, almost a leer of affection, like a living thing grown rich with the years.

It could have been, but for the Land-Rover, an evening in 1810, when the first Mannfred had brewed his special drink and sent it out in barges across the lake.

Except for one detail more.

The kicker in Marsh's watch was flicking angrily.

2

The three got out of the truck and looked around them. The Vat reared up into the evening sky, as fine an example of eighteenth century barn building as could be found in the country. It had started as a barn, and the first Mannfred, to turn it into a distillery, had fitted the inside to suit.

Tall firs surrounded it except on the lake side. The evening was eerily still. The grunting opening of a door towards the end of the dark building was almost a shock.

The three came to life. Mannfred grinned.

'Meet Jass Laver, one of my most reliable watchdogs,' he said. 'Jass, two friends of mine want to see over the Vat.'

'Yah, sure,' said Jass. He was a large cadaverous looking man, bent now with age, yet still his pale blue eyes were sharp and quick.

'Jass has been with us fifty years,' Mannfred explained as they went towards the open door. 'He looks on nightwatchmanship as the best form of retirement. Right, Jass?'

'Sure, yah, Mister Richard.' His unsibilated 'Yesses' were almost like yawns that split his bony lantern jaws. 'Bonus is tucking in now this minute.'

Mannfred went past Jass into the building and Mary followed with Marsh close behind. They walked into what could have been the cave of an ancient alchemist. The lights were few and hung from the high beams; a watchman's meagre amount of light. Great copper stills glowed redly in the lights, pipes snaked everywhere, gleaming with constant polishing. There was a rich warm smell of damped furnaces but no trace of any Royal G in the atmosphere. Wooden skeleton stairs zig-zagged up into the darkness of the roof rafters, joining on to wooden galleries, railed with heavy oak, polished black.

Mannfred led them past the giant copperworks and on to oak-walled tanks half-set in the stone floor. These tanks were open-topped, square in plan and lined with brilliant copper sheet.

'These are scrubbed by hand after every making,' Mannfred said. 'It's still the only absolutely sure way of cleaning. Not all your machines can do it as well yet.' He laughed.

They passed doors in the side wall where crooked windows looked out on to the lake. They came to copper and teak storage tanks with gleaming copper and glass fittings.

'Half the day's work must be in cleaning,' Mary observed.

'Just a little over, in fact,' Mannfred said. 'A fly in this ointment, dear, would mean a whole brew of Royal G to be tipped into the lake. Under the watchful eye of the Customs man, of course,' he added.

'You call him when you'rc distilling?' Marsh asked.

'He knows roughly the times, and he's here pretty constantly.'

'You know him well?' said Marsh.

'Intimately,' said Mannfred dryly. 'He's

virtually emperor of the still, king of the spirit. These storage tanks you see now contain the other ingredients that go into the pure spirit.'

Jass was loping slowly and silently along behind the little party. Mannfred went into a smaller room overlooking the lake, a place of old, high desks and papers and ledgers and books lettered 'H.M. Customs and Excise'.

The four went in. Mannfred closed the door.

Marsh looked at his watch. The radio indicator was still.

'There's no bug on just now,' he said quietly.

Mannfred nodded and turned to Jass.

'What's the trouble, Jass?' he asked.

'Couple of strangers out there, yah. 'Bout a half hour back. Seed 'em round by the crate yard. Thought it were shadows to start, but then I looked hard and it was men.'

'What were they doing?' Mannfred asked, and then turned to Marsh and Mary. 'You'll forgive me, just a minute?'

'Of course,' Marsh said.

He and Mary began looking round the room and out to the lake, apparently uninterested in Jass's report.

'I shouted to 'em,' Jass said. 'And like before, nobody answered. I don't mind good honest solid burglars and such. You can lay a beam on their heads. But this slinking and sneaking — I don't see what's the idea. Keep making you think something's going to happen, but nothing does. It gives me the jumps, Mr. Richard. I don't like it much.'

'Nobody tried to get it?'

'I heerd somebody muckin' with the doors to the loading bay. I goes there and hears en on t'other side. Then I shoots the bolts and opens the door, sharp like, and nobody's out there. Then Bonus, he don't help. Silly bit of a sack he can be sometimes, I say. Yah!'

'What did Bonus say?'

'He starts on about this old yarn about the man of the lake. You know, the old slimy green ghost they used to say comes up out of the water when somebody's going to die.'

'That old joke!' said Mannfred. 'Where

did he dig that one up?'

'It's so long I heard it I forgot it till he says it this very night. I says where did he get it, and he says in the book. I says what book, and he says the book what's with the Bible and Sherlock Holmes and Whittaker's Alluminack — all them books on the shelf in the apprentice room down there.'

'He's not a great reader, is he?'

'Only horses and the pools,' said Jass. 'Reads that kind o' dross all night. I never knowed him read a book that int horses or football.'

'Why did he suddenly pick it out?'

'Seems he didn't. Seems he went in there and it were lying open on the bench. And it weren't then when I went in there, when us took over tonight.'

'You mean somebody's been inside the Vat?' Mannfred snapped.

'Well, Bonus wouldn't ha' chosen that kind o' reading. That's for sure. Yah. It was just a bit queer feeling somebody had put it there, for he ast me if I did, and I says no, so he goes green a bit and says what somebody must ha' bin inside here.'

'Could they have been?'

'We did the rounds after everybody had gone. Looked everywhere like usual and the lavatories. Everywhere was clear. There wasn't nobody here but Bonus 'n me. Then this book comes out of the shelf on its own and opens itself at the page about the Old Man of the Lake.'

He left it at that, a strong eerie punch line.

Mannfred turned to Marsh.

'Know anything about the supernatural, John?' he asked.

'I'm a physical culture man. I deal in extremely earthy bodies,' Marsh said.

Mannfred turned back to Jass.

'You don't think the men you saw and heard were ghosts, do you, Jass?'

'Not me. I'm too scairt to believe in ghosts. Nightwatchmen and ghosts ain't a happy pairing. No. It was men. Men pulled that book out, too.'

'How did they get in?' Mannfred said. 'If you say men did it you must know a way they got in.'

'We had everything shut tight, like usual. You see, even I bolted that there door when we all come in just now. I'd swear the place was empty, save for us two and now us — one, two, dree, fower, five — us five.'

'Well, let's take a look round and make sure,' Mannfred said. 'Where's Bonus eating?'

'In the 'prentices' room. He didn't have any supper. His wife went off sudden. Somebody got ill. She was called out then.'

'Member of the family, you mean?'

'Aye, reckon so. Yah. Her relative, far as I understand.'

The four left the office room and began a quiet round of the building. Mannfred tested every door, every window. They were all secure. The Apprentices' Room came last on the tour.

When Jass opened the door the room looked empty.

'Hey, Bonus!' Jass yelled. 'Boney! What's that, then? Where are yer?'

'Just a minute,' Marsh said, pushing past. He looked behind the door.

Bonus was lying there, flat on his back, his hands upturned.

'Great Strorks!' gasped Jass coming round the door with the others. 'What's he got, a stroke?'

'No, he's just plain flat out,' said Marsh, kneeling beside Bonus. He tested the pulse. 'Quiet, regular. Pupils — ' He bent close. 'Gas.'

'There's no gas hereabout,' Jass said, blankly.

'Not that sort of gas,' said Marsh. 'I mean he's been gassed. Somebody came up behind him and smacked a pad round on to his nose. You can smell it. Also, there's a chemical stain at the side of the mouth here, and a streak of it at the side of the neck.'

Jass stood rock still.

'There wasn't nobody here but us five,' he said. 'And all was locked up, like you seen. Is he bad?'

'No. I've come across this stuff before. It knocks a man out, gives him pleasant dreams and he comes to with a head in ten minutes.'

'Ten minutes,' said Mannfred. 'Then the gasser must be here still. Somewhere.'

'We've been everywhere,' Mary put in.

'Only a minute or so ago.'

The silence of the place was broken only by the ticking of a clock out in the still hall.

Bonus opened his eyes. He was a small, fat man of around sixty, but with skin as smooth and pink as a baby's. He stared up at Marsh.

'Hey! What are you doing here? No one's allowed — '

He shot up into a sitting position, then seemed to realise something was wrong with him. He felt his head.

'Crum!' he grunted. 'Some beer that must 'ave bin. Cor! Tasties like a sewer.' He licked his lips and grimaced. 'I had a pint on the way. Bugler's Arms. Tastied all right then. Never would 'ave thought — '

'You were in here having supper,' Mannfred said, quietly. 'Do you remember anything happening to you?'

'I left the plastic stuff round the lunch meat,' said Bonus. 'It come out like strips o' plastic in me sandwiches. 'Orrible it was. I kep' picking the stuff out o' me teeth. Like eatin' wire. My missus wouldn't ever have left that on. But she went off to her sister's. Took sick — ' His eyes widened, but he shook his head as if whatever he had thought of was rubbish not worth mentioning.

'Did you hear anyone in here with you?' Marsh said.

'There wasn't anybody to hear. You lot was in the office. I heard you go down.'

'Did you smell anything?' Mary asked.

'Smell anything? We don't have no smells in this plant, that I tell you, miss,' said Bonus, almost angrily. 'This is clean and sweet, this place, and I tell you, miss — '

He broke off, his eyes got big again and he touched his nose as if to see it still stayed on his face.

'Remember anything?' Jass said. 'A funny smell with your sandwiches?'

'Smell, yes,' said Bonus slowly. 'Funny you should say that, I remember a smell, yes. I remember thinking, them pickles is off. I remember thinking, and then I don't remember thinking. That's how it was. I'd eaten some already in the sandwiches. Pottomaine poisoning! That's it!'

He let Marsh help him up and sit him on a stool.

'You've been doped,' said Marsh.

'What — like a horse?' said Bonus blankly.

'That's all he thinks on — horses,' said Jass. 'So it's a sign he's getting better in his mind. No, come on, Bonus, you old pod! Get your brain working. There must 'ave bin somebody in here with you. Somebody you didn't see.'

Mannfred went across the room and opened some of the old cupboards. There was a certain amount of workmen's property in them, overalls, boots, old gas-mask cases used as lunch bags.

The windows were all in one wall, overlooking the water. Far down the lake shore the small shape of a punt stood still on the water, an even stiller fisherman sitting in it. That was all in the silent scene.

The people in the room were quiet. Even Bonus stopped breathing to consider what had happened to him. The quiet, the absolute lack of activity gave the menace a stronger, more frightening quality than any active, frontal threat.

‘What about the police?’ asked Jass.

‘Don’t think we’d better do that,’ said Mannfred.

That was all he said about it. Marsh read into it a suggestion that calling the police indicated his own watchmen were inefficient, asleep on the job. He would not suggest that until he had to.

Having the police in would also undermine the confidence of his other staff even more. It would increase their early fears that something, somebody was creeping up on them.

Which, Marsh was sure, was the very purpose of the whole quiet disturbance.

He looked at his watch again. The kicker was still.

One puzzling feature of the bugging of this firm was the sporadic manner of it. Maureen had sent signals, but they had cut off. Signals had been radiated when the party had arrived at the Vat, but not since.

It then occurred to Marsh that this could be yet another underminer of confidence, directed now at any anti-bugging specialist who might be engaged to find out about any leak in the organisation. A system of automatic bug radiations, cutting in and out, laying a trail to nowhere.

'What do we do, then, Mr. Richard?' Jass asked.

'It's up to Bonus,' Mannfred said. 'Do you wish to prosecute for assault, Bonus?'

'No, I'd just as soon belt the beggar when I do sets me eyes on him,' Bonus said. 'Doped! Me! Cor! I'd best get me saliva tested.'

'Okay,' Marsh said and brought a leather wallet from his pocket. He opened it and took out a Cellophane envelope. 'Just touch this slide with your tongue.' He pulled a fine glass slide out of the sheath and held it to Bonus.

Bonus gingerly touched the glass with his tongue. Marsh slipped the slide carefully back into its envelope and the envelope to the wallet.

That done he took a small pistol from his pocket and handed it to Jass. 'Great Crump!' said Jass.

'It's a water pistol, extra powerful jet,' Marsh said. 'Listen to me carefully. For the rest of the night, stay together. Don't part as you did last time. Understand?'

Jass nodded, his bony jaw half-dropped.

'The pistol is loaded with marker dye that won't come off for five days,' Marsh said. 'So if you see any shadows, hit 'em with the jet. You can have several shots. Just a quick pressure of the trigger each time.'

Marsh signalled to Mary. She came forward with her big satchel handbag slung over her shoulder and opened the flap.

Marsh took out a flat tin box from the bag. He opened it and showed a glass compass dial.

'This is a small radar,' Marsh said. 'One of my own works. Now listen to me. I'll switch it on now, and don't touch the switch after. If, after we've gone, anyone comes near this room, a spot of light will show somewhere in the dial. That spot will show the actual position of the intruder from where you are standing. Mary, go to the window, please.'

Mary went round behind the bewildered Jass. The set came on and a spot of light showed on the edge of the dial nearest Jass.

'The middle represents you,' said Marsh. 'So the lady is behind you. Do you see?'

'Aye! Yah!' said Jass, with sudden blazing enthusiasm. 'Why, by gorm! One needn't ever do any watching at all with one of these!'

'What about the plant, Jass?' said Mannfred quietly.

'Oh, yah, that immediately come to me mind, sir,' Jass said quickly. 'I would do me round in case a pipe was to leak or burst, or something. Yes, of course I would, no doubt of that!'

The visitors left the Vat just before dark. Once in the Land-Rover, returning to the house, Mannfred said: 'You let the cat out then, didn't you?'

'I don't think it's much good trying to keep our purpose hidden,' Marsh said. 'This place is under careful surveillance, and so are you. They know where you got in touch with me, and they'll know, as you did, what we do to make a living. I don't think we own an element of surprise in this case.'

'That doesn't sound very cheerful,' Mannfred said. 'It seems to mean they have the access.'

'We have to find a trump,' said Marsh dryly.

* * *

LOHM building was quiet. The executives had gone their ways, the last lingering ones at the bar finally prised away.

Sheila cleared up, humming in a high pitched voice. She heard someone moving in the corridor beyond the open swing doors, but the building was open to all sorts who paid the fees and there was nothing unusual in that.

The man came in casually, doing up a cuff-link as if having dressed hurriedly. He smiled at her.

'Surely not too late?' he said.

'No,' Sheila said. 'If it was too late I'd have been gone hence hence. That is right, is it? I'm never quite sure if Shakespeare wasn't pulling my leg.'

'I was never sure, either,' he said, and looked quickly along the shelves behind the bar. 'A long lime and soda, iced.'

She mixed it.

'Now shove a treble gin on top,' said the man.

'You're new, aren't you?' Sheila said. 'Yet I seem to have seen you before. Somewhere.'

'Aye,' the man said. 'I'm here to lose a bit of weight. They say I'm too hefty for *Hamlet*. Just come to sign on and reduce.'

'You've seen Miss Shore?'

'I have that,' the actor said.

'You must be Jimmy Gaunt,' she said.

'I must,' he said. 'Nice of you to know.' He drank. 'Nice little fit-up you have here.'

'First-class junk,' she said. 'I saw you in that *Night after Night* picture.'

'That was a stinker,' Gaunt said. 'Never got off the grid. Sometimes I wonder how the producers get hold of this trash. Some friend, perhaps. But what kind of friend finances? I often wonder.'

He seemed a long way off from the conversation, thinking of something else, as if he was seeing something right away behind her.

'When do you pick up here?' she said. 'Tomorrow?'

'Not too soon,' he said, with a wry smile. 'I'm not keen to work myself to death.'

'Where is this *Hamlet*?'

'Edinburgh.'

'Soon?'

'Rehearsals next week.'

'What's the good of starting here, then? What you want is three days solid Turkish baths.'

'Try and cheer me up, sweetie. I'm down enough already without being trodden on. Don't stamp me in.' He smiled again, but he was still a long way away.

He finished his drink suddenly. A dramatic gesture, she thought; All is lost, I am the Next One to Die.

'Come to think of it, tomorrow, yes,' he said. 'One must face it eventually, why not now? Farewell.'

He swung his soft hat off, bowed and wandered out.

'He acts almost as if he *is* Hamlet,' Sheila said, and washed his glass.

She cleared everything then went out and along the passage to the office. The door was ajar and the desk light was on. The office was empty.

'Well, I don't know,' Sheila said, and then looked round.

The drawers of a filing cabinet were pulled right out, some files were on the floor together with boxes of tapes.

'Stagger it!' she snapped. 'It's a burglary!' She turned and ran out of the room, then stopped and looked up and down the wide polished corridor. 'Janey! Janey! Where are you? Janey!'

She pushed the door of the Ladies' Changing Room, but the lights were off in there.

'Janey!'

A queer little feeling of panic took her. The burglars might still be around, and it looked as if she were alone in the place.

She stopped and listened. There was a

faint running of water from one of the changing-rooms. That was all.

She ran to the end of the corridor and into the gym. The skylights let in purple light from the dying day and showed the big room empty.

Again the feeling of rising panic got her. She turned and looked behind her, then round the gloomy hall again. She had no longer the courage to shout.

She went to the wall switch, but stopped with her hand on the row of tumblers, too frightened to snap them down. As if she was scared of what the light might show.

She dropped her hand again, and then a cold wave of sense came over her.

'For Hell's sake!' she said aloud. 'What's the matter with me?'

She ran her hand down the switches. The sudden blaze of light blinded her, and then she saw there was no one in the hall but herself.

Somehow it made things worse. It would have been easier to have seen somebody crouching there. At least, you could either hit them or run. This way you had to go on looking, not knowing who was there or where they were.

She went back into the passage.

The empty quiet remained but for the sound of water running somewhere.

She ran on to the main entrance and out into the purple evening. All the cars had gone. Gaunt had gone. The world was empty. She felt like screaming.

She turned and went back into the corridor. The sound of the water seemed loud then. It seemed a deliberate attempt to saw at her nerves. She pushed the door of the Men's Changing Room, but it did not come from there.

Across the corridor she pushed the Ladies' Room door. The soft trickling was louder. Angrily she went in snapping the lights on. She came round the blind stand and went between the rows of steel lockers to the showers.

Then she stopped, shocked into a stillness that held her muscles almost in a kind of cramp.

'Heavens!' Her voice was a small scream.

She jumped forward to the end shower.

Jane Shore lay face down in the dished bottom of the shower. A tap, set in the side wall was running fast. Her face above the outlet seemed to be almost submerged.

Sheila dragged her back from the water and turned her on her back. She knew people could drown in shallow water. Jane was right out, her face and hair soaked. These things were all that Sheila did know. She had the vaguest ideas only of first-aid, life kisses, or how to pump water out of half-drowned people.

She gasped in despair, then turned Jane on her face again and put her knee in her back. Jane groaned, but nothing seemed to happen.

Sheila swore, then ran to a telephone under a small sound-isolating arch in the corner of the changing-room.

The phone was dead.

Heart thumping like a hammer she ran into the office where the switchboard was. Everything was plugged in. The main phone line was out, no sound in it whatever.

She swore again and ran back into the

showers. She bent down, wagged Jane's arms about then pressed her back, and some water came out of her mouth. Encouraged, she did it again.

Suddenly Jane gave an awful gasp.

Sheila jumped up. She felt as if she had revived a corpse and a creepy horror fixed her.

Jane sneezed, rolled over and then blinked up at the lights.

Sheila suddenly realised the water was still running. She went to it and turned it off desperately, as if this act would effect a final cure.

Jane sat up and shook her soaked head. Sheila knelt and put her arm round her shoulders.

'What happened, Janey? For goodness sake! You nearly drowned! Did you have a blackout? What happened?'

Jane felt her face as if to make sure it was still there, then shook her hair.

'I smelt something. That was all,' she said, steadying herself by taking long breaths.

'Was there anybody in here?'

'I didn't see anybody. There wasn't a

woman's class tonight.' She made a face. 'Gosh! My head! I almost feel I've been gassed!'

'Why did you come in? What was the matter?'

'I heard water running. Came in. Got as far as here then smelt something.'

'Where from?'

'I don't know.'

'There's been a burglary, too. The office is all roughed up.'

'Give me a hand,' Jane said. 'I'm as dizzy as a bell.'

Sheila helped her to her feet and she swayed quite a bit to start with. Then she bent towards a shower and vomited up a lot of water. Sheila held tightly to her arm.

'You'd better lie down,' Sheila said. 'I think you nearly drowned in there. But who did it? Was it deliberate? Or did you just fall there?'

Jane vomited again, then gasped and shook her head.

'I think you're right,' she panted. 'I must have swallowed a gallon. Oh, I feel awful!'

'It was that damn actor!' Sheila said angrily. 'There wasn't anybody else here. But — ' she glared at the wall, ' — you couldn't have been there long, could you? You'd have been dead in two minutes. So it couldn't have been him. He walked straight out after his drink. I saw he didn't come this way at all.'

'I'll sit down,' Jane said weakly. 'I don't think there's any more water in me. There couldn't be.'

Sheila helped her to a bench and she sat down and held her head between her hands.

'What actor?' she said.

Sheila told her with a lot of imaginative embroidery.

'He could have been a cover for whoever hid here,' Jane said. 'I was a fool to rush in like that. But I didn't think anyone might be here — '

'Wait a minute,' said Sheila, interrupting. 'Where were you coming from when you heard the water running?'

'I'm so dizzy I can't quite remember. From the gym, I think . . . Somebody was going out of the main doors. Right at the end of the corridor A long way off. Yes, I must have been coming from the gym — '

'Well, it couldn't have been the office, could it now?' Sheila protested. 'The whole place is standing on its head right now. That must have taken a minute or two and some noise, but all you heard was the water.'

'I'm not in the state of head to work out logic,' Jane said. 'Show me the office. I can't think why anybody would want to grab a lot of statistics of overfed city men and slim-mad women.'

'Well, they weren't looking for those for sure!' said Sheila. 'Hang on to me. You're walking with two jelly legs, girl, you ought to sit awhile — '

'I want to see the office!' Jane said. 'John will be mad when he hears.'

'What about when he hears about you?'

'It could have been an accident,' Jane said. 'I did smell something, but you know that people on the edge of a mental pause often do smell things. My brother smelt fried onions just before an operation. Now that just couldn't have been, could it? It was him, not the anaesthetist.'

'You were done,' Sheila said firmly, and then added a little doubtfully, 'somehow.'

They went into the passage and along to the office. Jane looked round the wreckage, then pointed to one tape box which was open and turned upside down on the floor.

'See if there's a tape under that,' she said. Sheila bent and picked up the box.

'Empty,' she said.

'That was the tape Mannfred turned on yesterday evening,' said Jane. 'The one that recorded why he had come.'

3

John Marsh and Mary came in while the two girls were still looking round the upset office.

Marsh put down his brief-case, stuck his hands into his pockets and scowled round. He did not look surprised. Mary put her satchelbag on the desk, and whistled.

'Things is moving,' she said.

'Seems they came after the Mannfred tape,' Jane said.

'And you,' said Sheila.

'What do you mean — and you?' Marsh snapped, swinging round to her.

Sheila told rapidly of Jane's near-drowning in the shower.

Marsh listened then dropped into the desk chair, still with his hands in his pockets.

'Get me a Scotch, Sheila,' he said. 'I'm all boots and no laces.'

'Anybody else?' Sheila said. 'Let me

guess,' she added and went out.

'It didn't take them long to hitch on to us,' Marsh said.

'Mannfred was probably watched here,' Jane said. 'Whoever is working on him at Trance followed. Possibly everything he does is watched now.'

'He doesn't give a hoot about himself,' Mary said. 'It's the workpeople he's anxious about. Fond of 'em.'

'Yet he must have a tyke or two in amongst,' Jane said dryly. 'This sort of haunting procedure can't be done entirely from the outside.'

Sheila came back with a tray of drinks. Marsh told what had happened at the Vat.

'Same stuff, same spot on the dial,' said Jane, dryly. 'Bonus and me. Is it the new-type chloroform-type?'

'Yes,' Marsh said and gave the name. 'Being used for smoking-out guerrillas out East. One sniff and pleasant dreaming.'

'With your head in the sink,' said Sheila, sharply. 'Do you think they meant to drown her?'

'No,' Marsh said. 'They just took the

risk it would. After all, it would have looked pretty much an accident. That knock-out gas doesn't leave any trace afterwards that can't be washed off.'

'I certainly had all the necessary washing,' Jane said, ironically. She had her head wrapped in a towel, turbanwise.

'You mean this was done to scare us?' Mary asked.

'What do you feel, dear?' John said, angrily. 'You're the witch of the party.'

'I get no impressions at all. No evil tang about this. The only reaction I got was a sharp one off Mannfred's wife.'

'I got that, too,' said Marsh. 'Only different.'

He took the tell-tale watch from his waistcoat pocket. The kicker was active. He got up, drank his whisky and looked round. The girls watched him.

'There's a transmission,' he said. 'But it isn't in here.'

He went to the door.

'Wait in here. I think this is another fake.'

He went along the passage towards the gym, holding the watch in his hand.

'What I think — ' Mary began and turned suddenly to the telephone switch-board.

The dialling tone was burring from the instrument there. Mary picked it up and put it on the hooks.

'In the excitement, I forgot to mention,' Sheila said. 'The phones were cut off.' She saw John Marsh passing the open doorway and shouted, 'I say again the phone was cut off!'

He stopped.

'When?'

She told him.

'And it's just come on again now,' Sheila said.

'Well, there's only one way to stop that phone — that's on the pole outside,' Marsh said.

He sprinted down the passage and out through the glass swing doors at the end. He came on to the lawn which fronted the building and looked up towards the looping phone line which swung out towards the road.

The pole by the roadside had a lump on it, just discernible against the powdery stars in the growing night. Marsh ran on.

The lump grew arms and legs and suddenly leapt down from the pole, disappearing behind the front hedge. Marsh ran as hard as he could go, but before he came out into the road a motor-cycle engine started.

He came round through the gateway in time to see a dark, swooping shape swinging off into the night, the only light on it a blue flame showing at the exhaust as the engine roared.

In a moment, the sound was a faint, dying whisper on the night.

Marsh went to the base of the pole, took a small keylamp from his pocket and shone it down. The marks of the man's feet showed on the trampled grass, but were too indistinct for any identification.

He searched around, but found nothing that might not have been tossed from a passing car, a cigarette packet, a chocolate wrapper.

He gave up and went back into the grounds. Two girls were at the entrance. Jane was standing on the grass, watching him.

He stopped close to her and looked at his watch again.

The kicker was strongly agitated. He walked about, using the strengthening and fading of the kicks to locate the bug.

It came strongest up against the wall of the triple garage. The wall was plain brick there. There was a drain gully at his feet. He looked up the pipe to the gutter.

'I'd say it's there,' he said, pointing up. 'Our spiderman must have been busy on the ups and downs.'

He went into the garage and carried out an aluminium ladder. He looked at his watch again. The kicker had stopped altogether.

'Interesting,' he said, and climbed up to the gutter.

He shone his small light into the guttering. A small matchbox-type transmitter with earwig aerials was standing upright in the gulley. He took it out and went down to the grass again.

'What is it? The usual?'

'Not exactly,' he said, putting the set to his ear. 'This one's ticking.' He turned to the garage and his workshop. 'Keep out of the way, darling, just in case the ticking isn't meant to control the radio transmissions.'

In his workshop he put the set on his bench and arranged two electromagnets on either side of it. He switched them on. He felt cooler when he heard the faint ticking stop.

He then set about opening the set.

It seemed a normal job save for the watch mechanism, which appeared to control the stop and start periods of the transmissions.

But the connections from the watch went to a minute junction box and there were two outputs from it, each leading into different compartments of shielded metal.

'Is it norm?' Jane said from the doorway behind him.

'Can't see,' he said. 'It's just possible there's a bit more circuitry here than normal, but the trouble is these units are so shielded and sealed up against interference they seal you out, too.'

'Is it another of those red herring

ones?' Mary asked coming behind Jane. 'Just sending signals for the fun of it?'

'The timing device suggests some such,' Marsh said. 'And there's no mike, which seems to clinch it. But the inside isn't familiar. There are two shielded boxes within where it seems to me one would do.'

'A double transmitter?' Jane suggested, coming into the workshop.

'For what?' he said. 'It's only transmitting a carrier wave, anyhow. There's no input for sound.'

'Is it sending now?'

'I have it switched off.' He went to a complicated direction finding set which he had developed. It gave position of transmitters and receivers, of radar transmissions, and also gave the frequency upon which such signals were working.

He switched the matchbox transmitter on with a jeweller's screwdriver, shorting out the watch control. Then he tuned his set until the signal from the little set showed a bright response in the cathode ray tell-tale.

'Same frequency as ordinary commercial bugs,' Marsh said. 'And this shielded component looks like that. But what's the other? Why double up the mechanism?'

'Are two transmitters working?' Mary asked.

'No. Only one. What I think — ' He broke off. 'Wait a minute! There's another signal coming in from somewhere else on the same frequency.'

He began to work his controls, searching for the location of the strange new signals.

'From where?' Jane asked.

'Out on the road!' he said. 'Can't fix it quite. Mary! Sheila! Nip out and see if you can spot a car or a bike. Don't let them see you.'

The girls turned and went out, keeping to the carpet smooth lawn.

Jane stood watching the tubes of the locator showing signals on their green faces.

'What kind of a signal is it?' she asked.

'Just a plain carrier wave. Like waiting for something to happen.'

'That's what the whole of this game

seems to be,' Jane said.

'With the exception of your bathe, which was serious,' he said. 'Ah! That's a clearer fix. I'd say two fifty yards westward down the road — '

The wave pattern of the outside transmission suddenly jerked in violent life on the tubes, like someone shaking a skipping rope. There was a scream from the loud-speakers, a constant, splitting noise and then suddenly a flash of light between the matchbox set and the locator.

It was intense, like a giant spark, but brilliant white. The locator exploded and suddenly the whole bench became a sea of magnesium fire.

Marsh shouted to Jane to back out and get extinguishers from the Land-Rover. He got one from behind the door, smashed the knob down and directed the hose at the blazing bench.

The brilliance hurt his eyes. Tears streamed down Marsh's face as he tried to keep the chemical playing on the fierce blaze, but it became more and more difficult to see. Clouds of greenish chemical smoke rose from the bench. The fire seemed to be beating the extinguisher by its very speed and ferocity.

Jane came beside him and directed another stream of chemical at the blaze. She could see. She had clapped on sun-glasses from the truck and she could discern where the heart of the fire was, which Marsh's streaming eyes could not.

She got it directly in the bright white heart of the conflagration and sheets of greenish smoke burst upwards, rolling along the ceiling towards them. But suddenly — almost as suddenly as it had started — the fire was killed into thick, choking smoke.

The workshop seemed plunged into sudden darkness after the glaring brilliance of the fire. The overhead lamps peered only dimly through the rolling clouds of the acrid smoke.

Marsh coughed, then pushed Jane out of the doorway.

'Come on out,' he gasped.

He shoved her aside, then switched on extractor fans. The workshop began to clear and through the whirling smoke

Marsh could just see the ruins of his locator, some of it still glowing red hot.

'Well, I certainly bought that one,' he said glumly, looking through the doorway.

'The second little case must have been a fire box,' said Jane.

'They must have realised we had stopped the watch,' he said, and coughed again. 'And so set it off by a radio signal. Very effective. Still, we're lucky. It only burnt half the bench. If it had gone off up in the gutter it would have burnt the whole garage, cars, workshop and all!'

The smoke began to clear from his lungs, but he kept coughing. At last he went out into the cool night air and the choking sensation went.

It was very quiet and still outside. The only sound was the soft droning of the fans pushing out thinning columns of smoke towards the stars from the roof vents.

'The girls!' John Marsh said, and ran lightly towards the gateway.

He came to the road and looked up and down it. A quarter of a mile away twin rear lights of a car showed on the bend. They did not move.

Jane came beside him.

'Is that the flame-thrower?' she said.

'Could be, though it's a bit farther off than the locator showed. It could have moved. But why stop again?'

He began to run silently along the grass verge towards the red lights. As he came near he heard the tearing sound of a starter turning an unwilling engine. The lights dimmed with each repeated effort to get motion.

Marsh slackened into a walk as he came close to the car.

Again the starter tore in, again the lights dimmed and still no response came from the engine.

He heard someone swearing in a high pitched voice, then the driver's door opened and somebody got out on to the road.

Marsh came silently up.

'Having trouble?' he said.

'Ah heaven, it's the darling man himself! Can you start motors? I'm after having a load of trouble with this beast!'

'Mrs. Mannfred,' said Marsh, hiding

his surprise. 'An unexpected pleasure. What happened?'

'Ah, here I'm cruising along and suddenly she fades on me and won't go.' She smiled at him in the starlight and he felt the warm shock of her presence again.

He turned from her as if to avoid the heat of his own feelings.

'Let's see,' he said.

He bent in and released the bonnet lock, then went round and shoved the lid right up and propped it. He shone his small torch in at the engine.

'Can you see anything?' said Maureen softly.

'Someone's screwed the HT lead out of the coil,' he said. 'How the devil could you do that while running along? Do you carry little men under the bonnet?'

She laughed, but he could hear a trace of uneasiness in the husky sound.

* * *

Marsh screwed the lead back into the coil and the car started.

'Why that's darling of you,' Maureen said as he got out of the driving seat. She threw her arms round his neck and kissed him with warm, soft lips that seemed richer than any he remembered.

In self-defence, he pushed her back and she laughed.

'Now I can be on me way,' she said, getting in. 'But where are you, in the middle of nowhere in the middle of the night, with no motor-car at all?'

'I live here,' he said. 'Back over the hedge there.'

'Well, why don't you ask me in for a drink then?'

'I will,' he said, 'but I was looking for some friends of mine.'

'A couple of women?' she said sharply.

'Indeed, yes.'

'They got in the car behind.'

'What car behind?'

'When I stopped a car stopped behind me, after a minute, and these two girls came along the road, and I see a man get out and they got in the car and then the car goes off, past me, never caring for me troubles.'

He knew she was lying, but he was not sure how much.

There was no one else in the car with her. It was not impossible but highly unlikely that the coil lead could have unscrewed itself so much as to fall right out. It would surely have ceased to transmit any spark a long time before that.

The unscrewing had been deliberately done to keep her there. But it surely couldn't have been done while she stood by, or she would have known what was wrong.

Then where had she been when the car had been immobilised?

'Yes, certainly,' he said firmly, 'come in for a drink. You can turn in a farm gate just along here.'

He got in beside her and directed the turn. As they came slowly back towards the grounds of LOHM he watched each side of the road carefully.

'The girls got in this car, you say?'

'Ah, it was a friend of theirs. I heard one call 'Hi, Joe'.'

'Joe?' he said, 'are you sure of that?'

'I think so. In here is it? Why, it's a

splendid palace of a place, too.'

She stopped by the main doors and they got out.

'I smell burns,' she said, sniffing.

'We had a little fire,' he said dryly.

Jane came up across the lawn.

'This is Mrs. Mannfred,' he said. 'One of my partners, Miss Shore.'

'Oh, very formal indeed,' Maureen laughed. 'I must be careful.'

'The girls went in a car with a man called Joe,' Marsh said and he took Maureen's arm and guided her to the doors.

'It sounds like a fairy story,' Jane said, with a hard little smile.

'You know what girls are,' Marsh said. 'Mad keen on fairy stories.'

'Well now, I'm not very handsome,' Maureen said. 'Where do you keep the wee place?'

'In the changing-room,' Jane said, and showed her. She left Maureen to fix her face and came quickly back to Marsh. 'What's this?'

'She says they got in the car just like friends.'

'It could have been a client they recognised.'

'That would make two coincidences, standing by the roadside out there at eleven-thirty at night.'

'Could she have sent that burn-up signal?'

'No. There's nothing in the car but an ordinary radio. I had a good look, enginewise, also.' He told her about the coil. 'So she couldn't have been in or with the car when it was disconnected.'

'Where was she then?'

'I can only think, in the grounds here.'

'Doing what?'

'We don't know enough about her to guess.'

'You said she had a bug this evening at the Trance house.'

'She did. Now it looks as if she was planted out on the road there to make us think she bugged us with the fire bomb.'

'Whose side is she on?'

'That's the big question. I don't much care to guess the answer now. Here she comes.'

Maureen came out of the changing-room, smiling and beautiful. If she was a spy against her husband, Marsh thought, then she was doing something very risky in putting herself right in the hands of the anti-spies Mannfred had hired.

For she would know the real reason for his coming to LOHM — if she was against him.

But would she if she wasn't?

Her effect on Marsh was almost fiercely emotional, which had the effect of tying his thoughts in weird knots.

They went into the lounge bar.

'My, this is a place. I do like rich places,' Maureen said, delighted. 'I'd be sooner coming to do my spare tyre exercise here than home.'

She laughed, took his hand and squeezed it. Jane turned away abruptly.

'I'm going to have a little of the Irish whiskey,' she said. 'It makes me burst into the tears for homesickness.'

'How long have you left home?' Jane said.

'Why, when I married my husband. 'Twas not all that time ago.' She laughed.

'I should be over with homesickness by now.'

'The man stopped behind you — Joe,' said Marsh. 'Was he stopped there when the girls came up?'

'He stopped behind me, a little ways back. Just there for a moment, I suppose, and I was a bit anxious, for you never do know for sure who it will be at night.'

'But nothing happened till the girls came up?'

'Why, no, nothing, nothing at all.'

'You were trying to start the car all this time?'

'In between swearin' at it.' She laughed again.

The phone went. Jane took it at the end of the bar.

'Did you see a motor-cyclist any time tonight?' Marsh said.

'If I saw one I saw twenty, for sure,' she said. 'There is some kind o' meetin', or some such.'

He gave her a drink, and she smiled with twinkling eyes into his as she spoke a Gaelic toast.

'Where were you going?'

'I was just wanderin' round,' she said, and the twinkle faded. 'One of these days I'll stop wanderin' and push her eyes right to the back of her head, I'm tellin' you for sure.'

'Who?'

'Clarice, for sure.'

Jane came back from the phone.

'Mary,' she said.

'Where?' Marsh said.

'Joe Hardwick's. Sheila's boy-friend, or one of the train of 'em. Photographer. They followed a car into Denford and lost it.'

'I'm going mad,' Marsh said quietly, and turned back to Maureen. 'Did you see another car — a third car?'

'There was a car ahead of me when I stopped,' she said. 'It was me slowin' down that made me engine stop. Slowin' down for him as on the bend.'

'You didn't mention it before.'

'I'm never a true, logical character, darling. Sometimes I remember a story right from the back to the front.'

He wondered if there was a tell-tale hint of nerves about the varying tone of her brogue. Sometimes g's dropped and sometimes they came out hard and ringing.

He turned to Jane.

'What are they doing?'

'Honking back. He's bringing them. Hardwick.'

They all sat down and lit cigarettes.

'Clarice gets on your nerves,' Marsh said.

'She gets on worse than that, darlin'. Worse, worse, worse. She bosses everything there. She's a bitchy beast.'

'What is she? The secretary?'

Maureen shrugged.

'Sometimes I wonder what. Where she starts, where she ends. She bosses everybody, me, Richard — everybody.'

'Why does he let her?' Marsh said.

Maureen shrugged again.

'Every strong man has some weak part. She knows what it is. I never found out.' She pouted.

To Marsh it seemed more of a kittenish, half-humorous grimace than any reflection of deep feeling. It was just one thing more about her that made her more of a mystery than ever. One minute he thought her transparent, then he found not transparency, but a reflection from what could be a hard, bright surface.

'She works closely with your husband?'

'Very much, darlin'. Hardly leaves him alone when he's there. Here is the report, here is the letter, here is the Lord-knowswhat. Here is any old thing just to keep you talkin' to me. I'd pull her old hair out, but I think it's a wig.'

'How long has she been with Royal G?' Jane asked.

Maureen looked at her in surprise.

'Why did ye not say with my husband?' she said.

'Because it's the firm she's with.'

Maureen relaxed, then laughed huskily.

'Well, yes, I never do think of it like that, then. It's because she makes me so mad, I think, and I want her to make me madder. Do you think I'm crackers, off me head?'

She looked appealingly at John Marsh.

'Yes,' he said.

'Well, damn ye then!' she said, and laughed again. 'I'd sooner be off me head than a fat old bitch like her and schemin' like a witch. If anybody's spyin' on Richard it's that overbusted old bag, and I'll not be sorry for any word I'm sayin'.'

And then she really let go. She let go every thought about Clarice that had come into her head and stayed simmering for weeks. Every hate, every burn, every little tiny scratch she had felt from Clarice came out in a gush of fury. She swore, she slandered, she built an image of horror and tore it apart.

And yet, through the terrible denunciation, the listeners knew there still remained the warmth of humanity in her for the hated one.

At the end she got up.

'That's for her ladyship,' she said. 'Wait for me. I'm goin' to be sick.'

She went out of the lounge.

'Boy!' said Jane, and whistled.

'I wish I wrote plays,' Marsh said. 'Get me another whiff of Scotch, dearest. I keep tasting that awful chemical in my throat.'

'In spite of all, I like her,' Jane said, taking his glass.

'In spite of what all specially?'

'In spite of her trying to seduce you.'

'You think that?'

'Yes.'

'So do I,' he said. 'And I feel like an easy fish. She's terrific. Can't think why Mannfred lets Clarice get in between.'

'That could be a key to this business,' Jane said. 'Clarice the jealous, possessive secretary, mad over him marrying some tart from Killarney — '

'Easy! Remember my feelings.'

' — could have been driven to selling the Mannfreds up to some outside firm. That's how it so often happens.'

'So often. But there are complications here. It's Maureen who's attracting all the suspicion right now. Jealous wife, not jealous secretary.'

'But does she know anything about Royal G?' Jane asked. 'My guess is she doesn't and couldn't care less.'

Marsh got up.

'Look after her,' he said and went out.

It was dark outside, but Maureen's car lights were still on. Marsh went and opened the passenger's door. The inside light came on. He pulled out the ash-tray in the nearside door. It was crammed with half-smoked plain cigarettes. They smelt fresh.

He shut it and went round to the driver's door. The ash-tray there had two cigarette ends, tipped ends, stained with rich red lipstick. He shut that, too, then closed the car up and walked across the grass to the garage.

The place smelt acrid still. He switched the fans off and went into the workshop to survey the damage. The bench was charred and seared with the bright fire that had burst from the tiny radio. His locator looked as if it had burst from the inside, its entrails were sprawled out over the bench.

'Nerve gas and instant fire,' he murmured. 'This smells of a chemist. A research man. Well, they use a lot of chemists in distillery by-product labs. Could be. Could be . . . '

The gas and the fire were the only two small details that looked as if they might link up. Nothing else did. The rest of the happenings might have been the disconnected ramblings of a lunatic.

Or the deliberate maze created by an expert puzzle maker.

The business of the three cars outside LOHM. How had that suddenly cropped up, and why? What had Maureen been doing there with a nervous man at her side, lighting and cramming out cigarettes as fast as his jags could let him?

Had he been in there with her while she had been stopped up the road? Who disconnected the coil? How, if Maureen was there? And if she wasn't, what in hell had she been doing? Spying on LOHM? What sort of sense did that make, when she had every legal and social excuse to walk in the front door?

The attacks on Jane and Bonus had been intended to scare, not to harm, though either might have gone wrong in some detail and turned into a police case.

The attack on Jane —

He came up short.

Could it have been *that* which Maureen had been doing while the car had waited up the road?

4

Joe Hardwick brought the two girls back to LOHM. It was then around 1 a.m. and Maureen, with encouragement from Irish whiskey, had said a lot, but it was all too personal to have much bearing on the Fear Makers at Trance.

Hardwick was tall, ginger, freckled, with protruding teeth and an almost constant grin. You had to look for the twinkle in his blue eyes to tell whether he was laughing or just grinning fixedly.

He knew nobody but Sheila, who introduced him round with a flick of the hand.

'Flickmaster Joe,' she said.

Joe's eyes twinkled. Marsh gave him a drink.

'What happened?' Jane asked him.

'There's me hauling up to light a smoke,' Joe said, turning his glass round and round in his hand. 'A car comes by me, very slowly — slowly enough to make me wonder what. Anyhow, he goes on by. Just on sidelights. Crawls the verge and then I see his lights reflecting on some car ahead near the bend.

'It all made me wonder what. So I got out and the girls came up, so we shunted after the car with the sidelights on.'

'The other car had no lights?' Marsh said, without looking at Maureen.

'The other car had no lights,' Joe said. He did look at Maureen, and there was some light in the eye exchange. Joe grinned more broadly.

'What happened when you followed?' Marsh asked.

'The drifter hooked on to our purpose. He shot away. I had some job to hold on, but he wasn't going wild. Just fast. Then we got into Denford and he double turned on us and went by going the other way. We just didn't stand a light of a chance then.'

'Did you get any number?' Marsh asked.

'Nowhere near enough,' Joe said, and shook his head. 'I wasn't even sure what it was. Thought it was a Jag, but Mary said it was an Aston.'

Marsh sat on the arm of Maureen's chair and smiled down at her.

'How did you forget the lights?' he said.

'For dear's sake, sweetheart,' she said, smiling back, 'I thought it was me battery wasn't man enough to start for me. So I offed me lights and tried then. 'Twas no good, either way, darlin'.'

If it was a lie it was good and reasonable.

She stood up and put her hand on Marsh's shoulder to steady herself.

'You know somethin'?' she said. 'I'm not in a fit state to drive meself back, now. There's a fine thing! You'll have to do it for me, darlin'.'

Marsh's eye flicked to Jane, then he stood up.

'Right,' he said.

Maureen beamed, kissed her hand to the others, then caught Marsh's arm and almost pulled him out of the room and into the corridor.

'She'll eat him,' said Jane.

When the couple got out into the starry

night, Marsh said, 'I'll take you. Leave your car. I'll send it back in the morning.'

'Surely, surely, there's still a smell of burnin' out here.'

They went towards the garages.

'We had a little fire. I told you,' Marsh said.

He got into a big Rover, pushing the far door open for her. She got in. Marsh backed out, drew round, then whispered off into the road. As he turned into it, Marsh looked along either way, but no car lights showed.

He turned towards Trance. She seemed to fall asleep in the deep seat. He thought she had.

She reached out suddenly and switched the lights off. He swore and switched them on again, slowing. She switched them off again, laughing. He got her wrist, and there was a brief struggle. He swerved on to the grass and stopped.

She flipped the back of her seat down flat, let herself go with it and grabbed him round the neck, pulling him down on her, laughing breathlessly.

'It's an old Irish game, darlin',' she

said, and started to show him how it went.

At first he resisted, but then his feelings got the better of him and he reacted to her lively enthusiasm. Either she was starved and desperate or she was the hottest thing he had found outside a blast furnace. He didn't even think how Mannfred handled such a ball of fire.

A car went by, slowly, it sounded, but neither took any notice. Something fell on Marsh's back, something light. There was a hiss, and then the car began to fill with white smoke.

'The hell!' he gasped, disengaging from her.

'It's being gassed we are, for Christ's sake!' she said in alarm, and grabbed him again as if to protect herself.

She stopped him getting out of his door. He reached across and opened hers. They rolled out together under his impulse and fell to the long grass. Clouds of the whitish smoke poured out of the open door and rolled lazily upwards to the sky.

His eyes were streaming. He could see

nothing of another car fleeing down the road.

She broke from him and sat up.

'It's in me eyes, for damn's sake! I'll look a sight now, for sure!'

He got up and wiped his eyes with his handkerchief, but when he cleared his sight the road was empty either way.

She just sat there, her eyes squeezed shut, tears sparkling on her cheeks.

'You turn your face the other way,' she said. 'I'm not fit to see, then.'

The car cleared, the smoke thinned on its upward trip.

'Tear gas,' he said. 'But a floating kind. That's new.'

'Do you mean you usually have such things thrown in your car?'

'No, but the ordinary variety holds the ground, heavier-than-airwise. And it doesn't smell like this.'

'You mean some little man's been making some for fun,' she said. 'Keep your face turned away and give me a hand up.'

He did, then gave her a handkerchief.

'Now what in the world would anybody

want to do that to us for?' she said.

'Have you got any jealous lovers?' he asked lightly.

'I don't know about jealous,' she said. 'What for? It wouldn't be Richard, now. He'd be out the car, in the door and throw you over the road and then go and pick ye up and throw ye back again. He's some fightin' man, is Richard.'

'It certainly wasn't your husband,' Marsh said. 'Can you think of anybody else?'

'Nobody whatever at all,' she said. 'Not a damn single one of anybody.'

'Who was the man you had in your car tonight?'

'Man?' She forgot her looks and flashed her eyes at him. 'What are ye takin' me for, a nymph or somethin'? Man? One a night's enough for me, and at the present, you're him. Now you take me on home. It's your friends I'm gettin' bored with, then. A lot of practical jokers, for damn's sake. Come on. Take me back!'

She got in and slammed the door, then hitched the seat up again. He got in the driver's seat. He went to start but the engine was still running. They went off, quickly now.

Nearing Trance a car came towards them and dipped very late. As it came up to go by Maureen gave a short cry.

'It's Richard!'

Marsh looked at the clock. It was then one-fifty.

He braked and looked back. The stop lights of the other car were flaring against the dark background of the forest.

Marsh stopped. The other car swung across the road, backed, then came on down towards them. He and Maureen got out on to the road. Mannfred pulled up behind the Rover.

He, too, got out and came up, his bulky form moving with strange lightness on his small feet.

'What the hell are you doing?' he said to Maureen. 'I've been doing my nut, thinking you had an accident or something.'

'I had a breakdown, darlin', but luckily it was near the gym place.'

'You dumped the car?'

'Surely I did. But at the gym, then. Mr.

Marsh is goin' to have it sent back.'

'Thank you,' Mannfred said, looking keenly at Marsh. Then he looked at his wife. 'You smell as if you've been in an acid bath. What in hell is it?'

'They had a fire at the gym. Just a little one, but it smelled awful,' said Maureen, getting her shot in quickly.

'A chemical fire,' Marsh said.

'Well, you'd best come home,' Richard Mannfred said. 'Get in.'

She went and got into the car behind.

'I was coming to find you,' Mannfred said in a low voice. 'There's been more trouble. Bonus reports there *must* be someone inside the Vat, but I'm damned if I can see how.'

'I'd better have a look,' Marsh said. 'I don't like the way this is going. That fire wasn't mine. It was started by an outsider.'

Mannfred watched him closely, his eyes bright in the starlight.

'They're on to you, then? Well, that makes things easier. I hate secrecy. It makes me feel guilty.'

Marsh gave him a cigarette.

'Also,' Marsh said, 'Jane Shore was attacked in the changing-room in such a way it could have been an accident.'

'Like Bonus?' said Mannfred quickly.

'Exactly like Bonus.'

He said nothing but smoked slowly, thinking.

'I didn't mean you to be dragged into violence,' he said at last.

'That's an occupational hazard,' Marsh said. 'But in this case I'm surprised it's hotting up so quickly.'

'Is that because you came in? Or was it timed to quicken just now?'

'Hard to tell. But they're splitting their attentions between you and us quite fairly.'

Mannfred turned towards his car.

'You go on down to the Vat. Saturn's the name tonight.'

Marsh nodded. The rear car moved off down the road towards Trance. Marsh let it go three minutes, then got into the Rover and followed.

He slid to a halt outside the Vat at two-seventeen. The bulk of the old place was black, but here and there yellow lights winked in the small-paned windows.

Marsh went to the door they had used that night and rang the night bell. He heard someone come to the other side and felt he was being peered at through some deceptive crack in the old door.

'Saturn,' Marsh said.

The only answer was a slipping sound of bolts. Then the door opened. Jass was in the passage holding the door.

'There's more trouble,' he said, and closed the door behind Marsh.

'What is it?' Marsh said.

'There's a bubbling in the pipes just started,' Jass said. 'I phoned the chief.'

'What happened before that?'

'Bonus saw somebody moving about up the gallery.'

They had come into the big hall now and Jass pointed up to the spidery woodwork of the ladders and galleries that rose away into the great darkness of the roof beams.

'How do you get up there?'

'Only from down here,' Jass said, pointing at the floor.

'When we left there was no one in the building but you and Bonus.'

'We didn't open any door or window anywheres after.'

'What about the radar I left you?'

'It just went all jazzy, like when the telly goes wrong.'

'Jamming,' Marsh said.

He looked at his detector watch. The kicker was still. There was no transmission taking place in or near the building.

'What about the bubbling in the pipes?'

'Means somebody's let air in.'

'How?'

'The air cock is up there.' Jass pointed up into the galleries again.

The big copper stills gleamed like fire in the lights, richly coloured against the old, dark woodwork of the place. Nothing moved, but higher up in thc empty air there was a gurgling sound.

'That it?'

Jass nodded.

'Seems like somebody must have known that cock,' he said. 'Nobody who didn't know what it was would touch it. There's eight up there. Only one lets in air, and it ain't marked. The engineer knows, so it don't need a mark.'

Suddenly Marsh saw someone moving on the high gallery. It was a man's figure which leant out over the railing and the blob of a pale face looked down.

'Nobody up yere, mate.'

Marsh relaxed. It was Bonus.

'Is the air cock off now?' Marsh said.

'Surely, yes,' Jass said. 'It upsets the brew, letting air in. There'll be hell to pay by morning.'

A bell began ringing.

'That'll be the chief,' Jass said and went to answer the door.

Marsh heard the bolts on the outer door, then heard the door slam shut. There was no sound of voices. No sound of footsteps approaching.

No sound at all.

He ran quickly, quietly back to the corridor. Then he stopped.

The corridor was empty.

Jass had gone.

Marsh ran to the door. The bolts were

drawn. He grasped the iron latch and suddenly a violent shock ran up his arm and right through his body. He could not let go of the latch. It held his cramped hand as if it had seized on solid. Marsh's jaws locked.

Then suddenly the shock ended. He let go. His muscles became flaccid, his jaws relaxed. The current had been switched off.

* * *

It was around that time the three girls were still in the lounge at LOHM. They were tired, but their minds were still wrestling with the problem of the night's oddities.

Then Sheila sat up in her deep chair.

'Do you know, I don't remember I heard Joe's car go,' she said.

'Why should he sit outside there?' Mary asked.

'He must have gone. We just didn't notice,' said Jane.

'Too busy nattering,' said Mary.

'I didn't hear him go,' Sheila said again.

'If he hadn't gone he would have come back,' said Mary.

'I didn't hear him go,' said Sheila again and pulled her long, lanky body out of the chair.

The telephone went and she answered it.

'Mannfred wants to talk to John,' she said.

'But he should be at Mannfred's before now,' said Mary, looking at her watch.

'Perhaps something delayed him,' said Jane dryly. 'Perhaps he was eaten on the way.'

'Jealousy flames in her scheming eyeballs,' said Sheila, then took her hand from the mouthpiece. 'I think he went to your house, Mr. Mannfred.' Then she put the phone back. 'He grunted a bit. Didn't sound pleased. Now,' she added, loping towards the door, 'whatever happened to Baby Joe?'

She went out. In a moment she came in again.

'Join me, girls,' she said. 'I feel something's going to scare my knickers off.'

'What's the matter?' Mary said, going towards her.

'His car's still there. Joe's.'

'Is he in it?' Jane said.

'I don't know,' said Sheila. 'And I'm not damn well going to look by myself, either. I've had one near-corpse already tonight. They give me the screaming mimis.'

The three girls went out and on to the house steps. The photographer's car was there, beside Maureen's. Jane went down the steps and opened the door of Joe's car.

'Nobody in,' she said.

'Look in the back,' said Sheila. 'And mind my goose pimples.'

Mary opened the back door.

'Empty,' she said.

'Then what the dickens happened to him, the wandering boy?' Sheila said, gathering courage to come down the steps.

They looked round in the darkness. Everything was still. The sudden click of the clock in Joe's car made them jump, it was so quiet all around.

'Nobody — nothing,' Mary said in a half-whisper. 'He could have vanished. He could have been vanished. Anything. I think it's time we called the police.'

'Suppose he's just having a snoozy over in the bushes?' Sheila said. 'We'd look a lot of nits, calling the gendarmes.'

'So far,' said Mary quietly, 'we've had assault, attempt to murder and arson. Isn't that enough?'

'You couldn't prove any of it,' Jane said. 'I think I must have been attacked. I don't *know*. There was just a smell of something John thinks was gas. You couldn't prove anyone outside the garage set it alight. That could be shown as an accident, too. As for Joe. He could be anywhere.'

'I'll get a beam,' Sheila said and went back into the building.

She came out again with a large spotlight and sent the beam cutting through the night all round them. There was nothing strange on the lawn, in the hedges, in the flower beds.

'Well, he couldn't have walked home,' Sheila said. 'The idea of exercise curdles his blood.'

'The garage,' Jane said, and went towards it.

Sheila sent the beam after her. She went into the yawning mouth of the place and switched on the lights. Two cars and the Land-Rover were there. Through the sliding doors at the back she saw the burnt bench.

The stillness made her want to shiver.

'Joe!'

Sheila's shrill raucous voice suddenly rang out. Jane started violently and swung round to look out into the night.

'Joe! Where are you? Joe!'

There was no answer but the echo.

Mary came to the doors.

'This is a deliberate game to shake us all stupid,' she said. 'You see nobody, you hear nobody, but things happen all the time. You know what? Soon we'll begin to suspect each other!'

Jane looked round the garage, turning slowly on her heel.

'Where did the man go?' she asked.

'He just walked off into the night. Artists do that sort of thing.'

They went out on to the grass again.

'It's a long walk from here to anywhere,' Mary said. 'For someone who hates walking.'

'What was he doing here? Out in the road when you found him?'

'Driving up from Trance.'

'What?'

'He's doing the pictures for their new publicity gambit. Didn't you know?'

'Nobody told me. So he was down there tonight?'

'Doing some shots in the house. Featuring the family business attitude, the family, the house. You know the touch.'

'Then his work should be in his car now,' Jane said.

She walked away to the car. Sheila was still calling and beaming the light into the darkness.

'Give us a beam here,' Jane said, opening the car door.

The roof light came on and showed the car empty. Sheila shone the beam under the seats and in every crack. They opened the boot. It was empty.

'Well, there's no camera,' Jane said. 'He didn't take you to his flat, did he?'

'Yes, but he didn't take anything in. It was just to use his phone,' Mary said.

'Why did *he* lie?' Jane said.

'Why is everybody lying?' Mary said. 'That Irish-woman. This Joe. What's the point? Mrs. Mannfred said a car was ahead of her. Joe says it was behind — behind *him*, no less. She said it was stopped ahead. He says he stopped behind her, then this other car came on past him.'

'They're both lying,' said Mary. 'But they can't be on the same side or they'd tally their yarns.'

'You're speaking of the man I love,' said Sheila. 'He's no liar. Not often, that is. Perhaps he just got confused about this third car.'

'What about his photographing the Trance house?' Jane asked.

'Well, now, see here, he might have taken his camera and walked off,' said Sheila. 'He wouldn't want to leave it for anyone to steal, would he?'

'That's too obvious an answer,' Mary said. 'It leaves just one question. Why walk off and where to?'

'That's two,' Sheila said, pouting. 'And I don't know either. Perhaps he was tight.'

'Well, he's gone anyway,' Jane said. 'Just a last look round.'

They searched the grounds with the bright beam but there was no sign of Joe. They went back to the building.

'I'm to bed, whatever happens,' Sheila said. 'I've had sufficient evil for this day.' She went to the glass doors of the lounge. 'I'll just flood out — or shall we leave all the lights on?'

'Might as well, till John comes back,' Jane said. 'I'll get my bag, though.'

She pushed the glass door of the lounge, then stopped.

'What's on now?' Sheila hissed.

'There's someone in here,' Jane whispered.

'Ye gods, what next?' Mary said. 'There can't be anybody!'

'In the chair. Look. Feet!'

She pointed to a deep arm-chair that was threequarters turned away from them. Beyond the front edge of it they could see two feet stretched out on the carpet as if the occupier sprawled in the chair as deep as he could go.

'The hell with this,' Mary said, and brought a small pistol from the pocket of her coat.

The three went into the room. The man in the chair was breathing heavily, almost snoring. They gathered round him staring down as he almost lay in the chair, breathing hard in deep sleep.

'Doesn't he look sweet?' said Sheila.

'How the dickens did he get there?' Mary said. 'And where's he been?'

Jane bent and sniffed the man's hair. Then she straightened quickly.

'Heavens! It made me feel sick again,' she said. 'It's the same stuff they used on me.'

Mary was looking back at the glass doors.

'Lock everything and search everywhere!' she said. 'Nobody could have got in the front. One of us was standing out there all the time.'

The windows were locked in the lounge. They went out and locked the main doors. Then they went round every door and window in the place. Every opening was locked and bolted.

'I closed them all myself before I went into the changing-room,' Jane said.

'Theoretically that should leave us all locked in with Nobody,' Mary said.

'I've got the creeps,' Sheila said. 'Why doesn't John come back?'

'That man Joe went out,' said Mary. 'You saw him go. We all saw him go out of the main doors. We came back in here. Nobody could have come in again without one of us seeing him pass the lounge door, and he couldn't have got anywhere without passing the lounge door.'

'So nobody came in,' said Jane.

'But how did Joey get back in the chair?' Sheila said. 'He must have been gassed and brought in. It's impossible.'

'It's been done,' Jane said. 'Get Trance on the phone. We've got to talk to John.'

Sheila went into the office and dialled. The other two waited in the passage.

'We'll all be crazy if this goes on,' Mary said. 'From lack of sleep if nothing else.'

Jane went along and looked in through the glass door at the sleeping man. The whole place was deadly quiet, the only small sound the soft burr-burr in the phone in the office.

'Hey!' Sheila yelled. 'Don't leave me alone!'

The other two went back to her. The burr-burr went on.

'Must be somebody there,' Mary said. 'He keeps a night staff for overseas customers. You sure you've got the right number?'

Sheila tried again. Still there was no answer.

'Queer,' said Jane.

'Everything's queer,' Mary said. 'I'm even feeling queer myself. It's this creepy business. You never see anybody — nobody threatens you. I'd feel better if somebody rushed in and shot the place up.'

'We can do without that,' Jane said shortly. 'I'd scream at the sight of anyone now.'

'There's not a squeak,' Sheila said. 'I'd better leave it a while.'

'What are we going to do with him?' Jane said.

'Let him sleep it off,' said Sheila. 'I mean, he is asleep, isn't he? Not poisoned?'

'Drugged,' said Jane.

'Didn't John say it lasted only a short time? Some minutes? Just a few minutes?' Mary said. 'Yes, he did. Five minutes. About.'

'That man's been sleeping there fifteen now,' said Jane. 'Also he went half an hour ago. If he's been kept quiet all that time it must be something besides that Brand X I had a whiff of.'

They went back into the lounge. The heavy, snore-like breathing still went on. The man moved, but only in a restless sleeper's way of changing position slightly. His head rolled and then was still.

Jane bent to lift his eyelid.

There was a terrific flash and she staggered back into Mary. The flash was so brilliant it seemed for a moment after that the room lights had gone out.

Sheila called out sharply. Mary fired a shot into the far corner of the room. Jane put her hands across her eyes and stood a moment before trying to see anything. When she opened them again, Mary was just going cautiously forward towards the far corner.

There was nobody, yet the flash had come from there.

'I can only see red splodges!' Sheila gasped. 'What was it? An explosion?'

'There wasn't a bang,' said Mary, and stopped dead.

They all stopped. On the lower platform of a small round table rested a camera with a powerful flash attachment.

Mary gave a sigh of relief.

'That's it. An accidental blow-off,' she said. 'Look! The flash is burnt out.'

'How did it go off?' Jane said. 'Who — ?'

She turned suddenly and looked back towards the chair.

'Get the door!' Jane cried.

Sheila ran to the door. Everybody stopped still. Silence fell again.

'What's the crunch now?' Sheila gasped. 'There's nobody here. Nobody went out — came in — nobody — '

'Somebody must have done,' Jane said,

and darted to the chair where Joe had slept. ‘He’s gone!’

The three girls stood still in the silence of the locked building.

5

John Marsh went back through the soft lit Vat to the hall of the big copper boilers. Bonus was running down the stairway to the floor.

'Jass — Where's Jass?' he panted.

'Gone away,' said Marsh tersely. 'Who had the dye pistol?'

'He did.'

'Let's hope he used it,' Marsh said. 'You'd better come with me. It isn't safe for you to be alone now.'

'What happened to Jass, for Pete's sake?'

'Somebody kidnapped him at the back door. I came back to see the same didn't happen to you. Follow me closely. Don't lose sight of me, whatever happens.'

'You bet not,' Bonus grunted, short of breath.

Marsh led the way down the corridor to the back door again. He put a glove on and then tipped the latch. He opened the door and examined the latch both sides.

There was no electrical connection. A simple shocking coil had been hooked up to the latch, then slipped off again, leaving only a very faint scratch from the alligator clip used.

Outside everything was still. The shadows of the trees rose blackly into the night sky like a forest of bayonets. Bonus reached back along the passage wall and snapped down a switch. A light over the door came on, driving back the ground shadows in an arc of fifty feet radius. The old cobbled yard looked like a sea of stone bubbles shining in the light.

But the valleys between them shone queerly.

'Water,' said Bonus, croaking in excitement. He pointed.

Water was swirling in tiny rivers between the stones, yet there was no sound of water running anywhere.

'Where could it be coming from?' Marsh snapped.

'There's a tap way over the yard. I don't hear it, though.'

Marsh stepped out on to the cobbles and looked all round him, particularly towards the trees. If anyone moved there the action would have been caught by the door light, but nothing did.

Marsh looked down.

'That's not water,' he said tersely. 'It has an oil content.'

He squatted and his nostrils twitched.

'Flaming hell!' he said in astonishment. 'It's Royal G!'

'Can't be!' Bonus muttered. 'Where would — ?'

Someone came into the range of the light. Marsh straightened, his hand dipped into his pocket and stayed there. A figure came out from amongst the trees round at the side where the gate to the loading yard was. Marsh relaxed and took his hand from his pocket again.

'Jass,' he said between his teeth. 'Where the hell did you go?'

'There was somebody round the back there. When I opened the door there was nobody, but I seed this one round the back, so I runned, too.'

'I told you not to split up!'

'Dint want him to get away,' Jass mumbled.

He was vague, almost stupid.

'Who was it?'

' 'Twas nobody but a tub. It were tipped over, rolling a bit. 'Twas no man but a tub.'

'That's where this liquor's come from,' Marsh said, pointing down.

'Ah, 'twas a tub of that reject,' Jass said, blankly. 'Taster said 'twere no good. Bit off.'

'When was this?'

'Yesterday arternoon.'

'What was the matter with it?'

'Taster said the blend was wrong.'

'Does that often happen?'

'Not in a month o' Sundays.'

Marsh walked off, treading the stone tops and came into the loading bay. He used his own small torch and shone it down on the overturned barrel lying just inside the gateway.

It had yellow chalk marks on it, indicating the contents were to be destroyed. Marsh shone the light round. There were two other tubs, similarly marked. Piles of empty crates stood around the loading platform. The double gates of the yard entrance were chained and padlocked.

Marsh turned back and came into the front yard again. Car lights blazed through the gaunt poles of the tree trunks, and the firm's Land-Rover came to the end of the drive.

Mannfred got out. He started to cross the cobbles and then stopped, sniffing.

'What the blazes — ?' he said.

'Reject tub overturned,' Jass said.

'Who took the bung out?' Mannfred said dryly. 'It wouldn't fall out!'

'What usually happens to a sub-standard brew?' Marsh asked.

'Poured away when the Customs man's here.'

'Do you get a lot of it?'

'Very little. Yesterday's was a disappointment.'

'Could it have been a coincidence?'

Mannfred looked angry.

'Nobody would be allowed to interfere with the process!' he said.

Marsh shrugged. It was no use trying

to make Mannfred admit the process was not so closely guarded as he believed.

Bonus told Mannfred about the air valve. Mannfred cursed heartily, then strode into the Vat to see for himself what had been interfered with.

Marsh, Jass and Bonus followed him, bolting the door behind them.

'Nobody could of got in,' said Bonus, almost in despair. 'Nobody, I says nobody!'

It certainly seemed very difficult for anyone to have got in that night. Though the identification of the air valve, one out of eight, signified someone who knew the distillery well. So if he knew the engineering, he might also have known the weaknesses of the doors and windows.

Yet Marsh had examined all these and could see no weakness.

He stopped by a great copper vat and watched Mannfred running lightly up the spidery, zig-zagging ladder to the shadows up amongst the roof trusses.

If the place was sealed, as it appeared to be, then nobody could have got in. Which meant whoever was interfering must still be inside.

Yet there had been nobody in the place but Jass and Bonus. Could it be one of the two?

As the thought struck him Marsh tried to reject it. The two men were old and had been with the firm all their lives. The firm was still looking after them at a time when a more modern set-up would have said, 'Get rid of them.' These things added up into old-fashioned qualities like loyalty and sentiment, but they still exercised considerable pressure in the world's affairs.

Their very attitude now, of watching Mannfred with baited breath, anxious that he would find no damage done, was in itself too genuine to be part of an act.

And where would such men have ever learned to act?

Marsh finally discarded the idea that it could be either of the watchmen.

Mannfred came down.

'Everything all right now,' he said breathlessly, and dusted his jacket down. His attitude suddenly stiffened and he looked incredulous. 'Dust!' he said, aghast. '*Dust!*'

The watchmen blinked at him.

'What in hell's name is dust doing in this place?' Mannfred cried. 'Dust! Good God! It was never heard of! Dust! I must be going mad!'

He covered his face with his hands.

'It's another trick,' he said hoarsely, dropping his hands. 'It's another way of wrecking. Dust!'

'What was the matter with the reject liquor?' Marsh asked.

'The blend was wrong.'

'But surely your blender couldn't make such a mistake suddenly?'

'He did yesterday.'

He explained there had been an over strength of spirit which had upset the balance.

'Could it have been introduced by interference with the mixing valves?'

'No.'

'Or by the actual strength of the spirit that was being introduced?'

Mannfred stared.

'It's possible,' he said. 'It must be

checked in the morning.'

'What did you think happened?'

'I thought Benson was off-colour. Ill. Shouldn't have been in charge of the blending that afternoon.'

'Did he seem ill?'

'He seemed very worried. I spoke to him but he said everything was all right. You remember I told you there has been an atmosphere of unusual tension in the Vat these last few days. It wasn't unusual for that sort of thing to be catching.'

'It never struck you that the fault in the blending could have been due to interference?'

'I put it down to a mistake due to worry. It was the obvious explanation. I suppose I myself was too worried to think of another reason.'

He turned to Jass.

'Brew some tea, Jass,' he said. 'We'll stay with you till daylight. Can't let you risk any more tricks.'

The watchmen went off into their staff-room. Mannfred sat on the foot of the spidery stairs.

'You had Hardwick at the house

tonight?' Marsh said, offering cigarettes.

Mannfred paused with his fingers on a cigarette.

'Hardwick?' he said, frowning. 'Who's Hardwick?'

Marsh flicked his lighter and offered the flame.

'The photographer,' he explained, showing nothing of his surprise.

'Oh yes. He's doing the pictures for the new ads. That's right. I couldn't think who you meant for a moment. But he didn't come tonight. It was last night.'

'Last night?'

'The night I called on your help. He was here after I got back.'

'And he hasn't been since?'

'Not that I know of. I'll ask Clarice.'

'She's not here now?'

Mannfred laughed shortly.

'Not now. There's somebody on, though. Betsy. I think I told you.'

The first grey of dawn showed in the small panes of the windows.

'I'd like to ring up my place,' Marsh said.

'There's one on the wall over there,'

Mannfred said. 'Call the house. Betsy'll give you a line.'

Marsh went to the extension phone. He pressed the calling button and waited. He pressed again.

'Nobody's answering,' he said, looking round.

'Give it a good triple buzz,' said Mannfred. 'She may be dozing.'

Marsh buzzed as advised, waited, then shook his head.

'No answer, but the juice is on. It isn't cut.'

'Let me,' said Mannfred, getting up.

He tried. There was no answer.

'I'll blow her up!' he said, scowling. 'Try again later.'

Jass came in with some tea. It was drunk gratefully. The men were beginning to realise what a long night it had been. A night of stupid, trivial distractions that caught the nerves and set them jangling. A night of shadows and things that almost happened, yet didn't quite.

But mixed in with these ghosts of alarm there had been solid, definite attacks. Gassing, arson, the tear bomb in the car.

Marsh was determined to let these go by for the moment. To call the police would show a weakness he did not want to let the enemy suspect.

He gambled on the possibility that, if the enemy knew he was going to fight on his own, he would grow more bold and take the chance of coming into the open.

If the police were called in, he would naturally shrink further back into the shadows, possibly cut his activities altogether for a long time.

Then, when the alarm died down, he would start again with an even greater advantage than before.

After the tea was drunk, Mannfred tried the phone again. There was still no answer.

'Let's get up there,' Mannfred said shortly. 'You be all right now, Jass? It's daylight.'

'Aye,' Jass said.

'I'll be back before the day starts.'

'Aye,' said Jass.

Marsh and Mannfred went out, got into the truck and sped back up the pine track to the big house looking down on the lake. The first golden streaks of the sun were reflecting in the big east windows.

Mannfred led the way into the house and through a doorway on the right of the hall. They went into a small office with a phone switchboard, two tables, two desks and a number of chairs.

No one was there.

Mannfred swore.

'Make your call,' he snapped. 'I'll find the silly bitch!'

He went out. Marsh got through to LOHM. Jane Shore answered.

'You asleep?' he said.

'Are you joking?' she said curtly. 'It's been an absolute nightmare here. Vanishing tricks, man-who-never-was — the lot!'

'Why didn't you ring?'

'We tried. No answer there.'

'How long back?'

'Two hours. Quite that.'

'What happened?' He listened as Jane spoke quickly, very shortly describing the events of the weird night.

'The same trick was played down at the Vat,' he said. 'The place is apparently sealed yet somebody gets in and out. There may be secret passages at the Vat, but I'm damned sure there aren't in our place!'

'Then we have a first-class illusionist somewhere.'

'Two,' he said. 'It happened with you and with us at the same time.'

'It's not hypnotism?' she said.

'It's too early to say,' he said. 'There are such tricks, but whether you can play them on a number of people of such experience as ours I wouldn't like to say. What I — '

Mannfred came in behind him, his face white, shining with sweat.

'Come with me! Quick!'

The man's distress was shocking. Marsh said: 'Call you back!' and rang off.

Mannfred turned and led the way out. He ran lightly up the wide, thickly carpeted stairs, turned at the top and entered a huge bedroom. There he stopped.

Marsh went into the room.

Maureen was lying face down on the bed, breathing hard in a drunken sleep, a pistol gripped in her right hand.

Betsy, the telephone girl, lay crumpled on the floor, blood matting the back of her fair head where a bullet had shot the life out of her.

Mannfred was looking at Maureen, his lip trembling slightly, his eyes shining with the start of tears. Then he pulled himself together and turned his back on Marsh.

'What now?' he said, huskily.

* * *

Marsh looked carefully round the room, then at his watch.

'She was tight,' Mannfred said. 'You know that. It must have been an accident.'

Marsh said nothing. He went to the bedside table. There was part of a glass of water there. He picked it up and sniffed it.

'Raw spirit,' he said.

Mannfred looked startled.

'Let me see,' he said and took the glass. It did not take his expert senses a second to tell Marsh he was right. 'How the hell did it get up here? It never gets out of the Vat.'

'Is it ever used like that?'

'No. It has to be broken. That was used as a knockout drop. It must have floored her straight away.'

'Straight away,' said Marsh quietly. 'Have you seen the gun before?'

'I gave it to her. I never knew there were any bullets for it. It was meant as a scarer, in case somebody broke in any time.'

Marsh went to the dead girl.

'It looks like a twenty-two, same as the gun.' He looked round. 'She must have been looking out of the window. Were there any feelings between these two?'

'There was a rumpus,' Mannfred said. 'It was over a person, but who, I don't know. Maureen is very free spoken when she likes, and not when she doesn't.'

'Was it very bad feeling?'

'Maureen's feelings are hot. I wouldn't say they were bad because they don't last that long.'

'When did the rumpus take place?'

'Last night. That's why she went off in her car. I thought it was to simmer down. When she didn't come back I thought she'd boiled instead and smashed up somewhere.'

'Last night,' said Marsh. 'So someone might assume this was part of the rumpus?'

'Why should she shoot, anyway?'

'Why should she shoot the girl in the back?' Marsh said. 'It doesn't sound like a wild Irish revenge to me.'

'I'm too dizzy to think,' Mannfred said. 'I'll get the police.'

'There's plenty of time,' Marsh said quietly.

Mannfred turned to him.

'What in hell do you mean?'

'Don't rush into anything,' Marsh said.

'Why not?'

'Because it's what you are meant to do. Maureen didn't shoot that girl. Put that supposition first in your mind. Put it that this was a plant, a frame-up, a picture for the police. If you don't suspect it wasn't Maureen, then you'd call the police. Whoever fixed this then sits back, his job done for him.'

'Well?'

'But if you don't call the police at all, he'll be stewing in his own alarm, wondering what the hell has gone wrong. Once he thinks that, he'll come back.'

'You think this is another part of the game?'

'It's a bit of a coincidence if it isn't.'

'No. I don't believe they'd try that. It's going too far. It's more likely there was some quarrel, a struggle and the thing went off.'

'See if you can bring your wife to,' Marsh said. 'Though I think it'll take some doing. The best way is to shove her in a bath. The heat will drag out some of the alk, and a cold shower might do the rest.'

He unhooked the flaccid fingers from the pistol.

'I've got to call the police!' Mannfred said.

'Why not hear what she says first? After all, you can't do anything for this girl. She's been dead two hours or more.'

He looked at his watch again.

'I don't know what to do,' Mannfred said, in despair. 'I ought to get the police. What am I doing, listening to you?'

'You asked me to advise!'

'But this is murder!'

'How do you know?' Marsh's eyes were sharp and cold.

'That's what they'll say, after the row between them, and getting bullets for the gun from somewhere — '

'Who was the row about?'

'I told you, I don't know!'

'Give her a chance to speak first. The identity of the person could make the difference between this being a murder and an accident. Give her the chance.'

'I must call the police!'

'Why? It isn't the law you should do it right away. Give her a chance.'

Mannfred stood in the doorway, breathing hard. Suddenly he gave in. He went to the bed, took Maureen up and carried her out into the corridor.

Marsh looked round the room. The french windows to the balcony had been open all the time. The bright new day streaming in made the dead girl look more horrible and yet less real.

Marsh turned his back quickly, walked out of the room and shut the door. The sound of running water came from the open door of a big bathroom next along from the bedroom.

Marsh walked towards it.

'Can you prop her up in it?' he said.

There was a heavy splash and then the sound of Mannfred's hard breathing.

'Yes. She's dead cold out. Good as poison, that stuff,' he called breathlessly. 'What's happened?'

'Just fix her and come out,' Marsh said.

He walked silently back on the soft carpet to the bedroom door. He listened there. The running water stopped. In the distance a cock crowed, and that was all. He looked at his watch again.

The kicker was going. As he watched it the activity grew less, as if the transmission it received was drawing farther and farther away.

Mannfred came out, wet and hot.

'What's the matter?'

'I'm having a wild guess,' Marsh said.

He held his breath a moment, then

turned the handle and opened the bedroom door. Mannfred looked over his shoulder.

'Good God!' he said.

Marsh walked in. He looked all round the room and behind the door. He opened the built-in cupboards and closed them again. Last of all he went out on to the balcony. It was long and fronted six windows like this. No others were open. Marsh turned back into the room.

Mannfred leaned against the door, wiping his sweating face.

'What bloody game is this?' he rasped.

'Better go back and see she hasn't slipped,' Marsh said.

'Yes.' Mannfred went quickly out.

Marsh looked round the empty room where, ten minutes before the corpse had lain on the carpet. Now there was no body but Marsh's in the room.

Now it was Marsh's turn to wipe his hot face.

Mannfred came back.

'She's safe enough. There's not much water — ' He looked round. 'What was it? A hoax? For heaven's sake, surely — '

‘The girl was dead,’ Marsh said. ‘You saw that.’

‘But what’s happened to her? Where is she?’

‘The murderer took her away.’

‘This is crazy, or I am.’

‘See if you can bring your wife to. She might be able to make it a bit more sensible.’

⋆ ⋆ ⋆

‘They’ve been playing the same game over there,’ Jane said.

‘I’m getting sick of these vanishing tricks,’ Mary said. ‘Where’s Sheila?’

‘Asleep. John’s going to ring back.’

They were in Jane’s flat above the LOHM offices. The day was dawning.

‘It’s been one hell of a night,’ Mary said. ‘I can’t make a single sensible thing out of it.’

‘That’s part of the idea. It seems to be working. If I were Mannfred I’d feel like giving in. After all, he’d get paid for selling out. It isn’t as if it’s a dead loss proposition.’

'He won't sell. It's his. It's been his family's for generations. I wouldn't sell something like that.'

'It's old-fashioned jazz right in the middle of a sea of computerised callouses,' said Jane. 'It doesn't seem to stand much chance. I wish — '

The phone cut in. Jane answered and switched through an extension.

'Okay, John. We're on loud and tape.'

John Marsh told them what had happened in the bedroom.

'I think it was meant to be one of the faked accidents,' Marsh said, 'like yours in the changing-room, but this one slipped and went too far.'

'Can Maureen say anything?' Jane asked.

'He can't bring her round. We're fetching a doctor. It might be dangerous, that amount of raw alk, though I confess we didn't think of that till his attempts failed.'

'She's used to a fair amount,' Jane sad dryly. 'Still, when the scene was so set for a conviction of the fair lady, why suddenly panic and unset it?'

'There must have been some detail which didn't ring true, which the police might have spotted. That thing could be ammo. Can you check up the twenty-two ammo in the office safe? Now?'

'Mary's going,' Jane said. 'You think it came from us?'

'I'm pretty sure. That would hinge up. The row with Betsy, going out alone, coming to us, knowing we had shots in the locker, getting some, going back, shooting her. It makes a clean little story.'

'Where does it fall down? Don't forget she could have been around here when the office was raided. Her car was outside and she wasn't.'

'I can't see where it falls down, mate,' he said, tiredly. 'But it must do or else the body wouldn't have been snatched.'

'If you say you were bugged in the bedroom, then it might be something that you said which persuaded them the game wouldn't go through.'

'If it was, I have on the minitape, so we might be able to trace it from there.'

'You had it running all the time?'

'From the time we got into the

telephone-room here. Look, Jane, I want you to go into Betsy Burn. Mannfred has her address as Bank Flats, 6 Carnstead, no next of kin. Take Mary, be careful, pose yourselves as a couple of BBC audience measurers. That always goes good and they haven't been round for a while, real ones, I mean.'

'Right, John. Here's Mary.'

'Hallo, John,' Mary said, slightly breathless. 'There are seven shots missing, according to the log book. Twenty-twos. The rest of the box was overturned. I had to gather them up from all over the safe. Looks as if they were snatched in a hurry.'

'That's one end sealed,' John said. 'A bit late, but closed, anyway. All seven are in the gun, one fired. From what I saw of the girl's head, it was fired close to. It would have to be to kill anyone with that size bullet.

'I'm hanging on here for the time being. If you get anything, ring me. But don't say anything of importance anybody else can understand. I'm getting very nervous about this set-up.'

At that moment Sheila, wild haired and eyed came into the room, hugging about her a dressing-gown that hardly reached to her pyjama knees.

'I hate to be hysterical,' she gasped, 'but there's a dead man out on the lawn. Why the hell doesn't somebody do something?'

Her voice ended in a scream.

6

'What's the matter there?' John Marsh's voice snapped from the telephone loud-speaker.

'It's Sheila,' Jane said. 'She says — Wait a minute!'

'There's a dead man out on the lawn!' Sheila yelled.

'Are you sure?' Marsh barked. 'It sounds crazy to me!'

'It does to me, too!' Sheila cried. 'Everything's gone crackers. I've had enough of this! Let me get out of here — when you've got that corpse away,' she added quickly.

Jane and Mary were at the window. By the corner of the garage the body of a man lay sprawled on the fine grass close by a line of bushes which ran up to the road hedge. He would not be visible from the driveway or the car park in front of the LOHM building.

'How long has he been there?' Mary

said. 'Who is he?'

'My God!' Jane whispered. 'It's not Hardwick, is it? That isn't how he disappeared?'

'Don't call anybody until you're sure he's dead!' Marsh said. 'I've had one of these uproars already and it looks like they're intended to involve us. Me, you, and Mannfred. Go easy. Go and make sure first.'

'I'll stay here by the phone,' Sheila said quickly. 'You signal up to me from down there. I'll pass it on.'

Mary and Jane went out. Sheila watched from the window. The body was quite still. It had not moved since she had first seen it, several minutes ago.

The two girls appeared on the lawn below. Sheila grew tense and watched them as they went closer and closer to the body. They stopped. Sheila held her breath.

Mary turned, went into the open garage and came out again with a radiophone from the Land-Rover, LOHM's private communication system.

Mary's voice called out in the room

behind her and Sheila started violently until she realised it was the loudspeaker in the wall above the telephone, which still hung free.

'Well?' Marsh's voice said.

'It's the actor man, Hamlet,' Mary said huskily.

'Dead?' Marsh asked sharply.

'Jane's just looking.'

There was a pause. Jane and Mary spoke shortly to each other, too quietly for words to be carried by the phone.

'I'm not sure about this,' Jane's voice said suddenly.

'You can tell if the man's dead or not?'

'I can't trace a pulse,' Jane said, 'but there's no sign of any injury and there's one hell of a smell of alcohol.'

'You mean he might be drunk?' Marsh said.

'I don't know. Not just ordinary drunk. He looks very bad. I think he could be dead.'

'I'll come back,' Marsh said. 'Don't do anything.'

In the sudden silence that fell in the grounds Mary and Jane heard the sound of a car approaching. It turned, with a faint clinking sound, into the drive and came slowly down. Both girls stood forward to draw attention from the man sprawling on the grass, though they felt sure he would not be seen from the drive.

The small pick-up, back piled with wire bottle crates, clinked to a stop by the side door of the building. The milkman got out, whistling a mournful dirge, and took some full bottles from the crates. He whistled his way to the door, put four bottles on the step and started back again.

Then he saw the girls and stopped whistling.

'Up earlywise, then,' he called out.

'Too nice to stay in bed,' Mary said.

The milkman looked up past his pick-up to the road gates which were wide open.

'There's a car out there, parked on the grass,' he said. 'Still got 'er lights on. Nothink to do with you, then?'

'I don't think so,' Mary said.

'Best tell the police, I s'pose,' the man said, thoughtfully.

'I'd wait,' Jane said quickly. 'It could be somebody gone into the farm across the road.'

'I just been there,' the milkman said. 'Nobody about. Dunno why they takes farms and then doos no work on 'em. Lying abed this time o' day! You never see'd that, not in the old days, lyin' around useless. It's lettin' your own cash roll down the drain, that is. You got to look arter things farmwise. No good to leave 'er to overgrow, like. You has to work an' work an' work. If you doos that you can get a livin' but be beggared if you can doin' nothin'.'

'No, I suppose not,' said Jane, wishing desperately the man would go.

But instead he leant on the open door of his little truck and proceeded to discourse on the running of farms.

'For heaven's sake,' Mary whispered. 'Get rid of him!'

'How?' Jane hissed.

'Take stock, now,' said the milkman. 'There's beef and money in that, but then they changes the subsidy over to milk, and then they changes it back again to beef and what with that and doublin' tatey production, and then orderin' less of it, why a farmer today don't know his backside from his elbow.'

'Heavens!' Jane groaned under her breath.

The milkman straightened, then leaned in a new position on the side of the pick-up.

'Take arable, then,' he said.

'Oh no!' Mary whispered almost in prayer.

'There's confusion for a man, then. Rotate the crops, they says, and then they tells you what to put in, only they get the charts mixed up and there's you planting same ruddy thing as what was there last year and year afore that, on account of it's all done in an office where the geezer don't know an ear o' wheat from a cow's tail but goes by some book written by some other geezer in London who never even mucked out a cowhouse and don't even know where the muck comes from.'

'For the Lord's sake!' Jane hissed, smiling in a forced sort of way.

'Take manure, now,' said the milkman, settling into a more comfortable position. ''Twas the day when you had a good dung and spread en around proper, but now you gets only sacks full of smelly dust as what has no semblance whatsoever to the droppings of a sound animal, which is the basic of requirement in the farm, then.

'Take, for instance, all this assin' about with pestilentialcides, now. Take that, for muckin' about with a sound bit of redistiribution o' nature. There's an interestin' thought, now — '

He looked in the car cab suddenly.

'Great dungspreaders! Look at the time then. I must on me round.'

He got in, swept round in a circle on the tarmac and steamed out into the road.

'What about the car out there?' Mary said.

'I don't know about that,' Jane snapped. 'Let's get this — '

They turned and went back round the end of the bushes to where Hamlet had lain.

He had gone.

Jane uttered an unbecoming but justified oath. Mary started peering under the bushes, though she knew she would find nothing.

Jane shouted up to the flat window.

'Sheila! What happened? What happened?'

Sheila opened the casement.

'What happened when?'

'Just now. Look — '

Sheila gave a short scream.

'Eeek! It's gone! Did you do it?'

Jane didn't bother to answer.

'What kind of car did Hamlet have?' she called. 'Did you see?'

Sheila told her. Mary went quickly to the gates and out to the road. A car of that type was stacked on the grass at the roadside, lurching slightly as if about to topple in the ditch. The lights were on.

Mary went along the grass to it, opened the door and turned the lights off. As she did it she saw the engine temperature read hot. She shut the door and went back into the grounds.

Marsh drove in two minutes later.

He listened bad temperedly to the story.

'It's a deliberate shake-up, meant to put us out of business as well as Mannfred,' he said. 'There can't be any doubt of that now.'

'I'm not sure this man was dead,' Jane said. 'He could have been nearly killed with alcohol — '

'That happened at Trance. The raw spirit was put in Maureen's glass. Obviously, this was the same stuff. A near lethal knockout drop. Very easily disposed of to anyone who drinks a good deal of spirits.'

'Was it a fake murder at Trance, too?' Mary said.

'No. The girl was dead. There was no possible mistake about it. The body was snatched, like this one. But this second effort might have been a double up of the first, perhaps to make us think the girl wasn't really dead either.'

'You did examine?' Jane asked.

'I did. Yes. She was dead.'

Mary put a hand to her head.

'Let's get inside, have some coffee,' she said.

As they began to walk to the main doors she added: 'That car was hot. It had been run some little while ago.'

'It's been light two hours,' Marsh said.

'Then the car was running after that,' she said. 'I tapped the gauge to make sure it wasn't stuck.'

'So somebody turned on the lights to attract attention to it,' said Marsh. 'Yet you say it was empty?'

'There was nothing personal in it. Might be a hire car.'

'Did you hear anything, Jane, when the milkman was here?'

'Coudn't hear anything but that awful droning voice,' Jane said harshly.

'We didn't expect anything to listen to — not from behind,' Mary said.

They went into the building and upstairs to the kitchen. Sheila was already getting breakfast together.

'Well, what now?' Jane said. 'We're pretty well forced to have the police in.'

'Mannfred won't have it. He wanted to,

at the first shock, then changed his mind,' Marsh said. 'He points out that if they come in, the whole thing will be public and we shall have lost our case.'

'Why?' Sheila said.

'Because the details will leak out about the spoilt brew, interference at the Vat, and public confidence in the goodness of Royal G will rock. That will end the business.'

'But what about us?' Jane persisted. 'There's been arson, an attack on me, a photographer snatched, a man near dead stacked on the lawn — '

'And no proof that any of these things ever happened,' said Marsh.

'Arson? You can see the damage!' said Mary.

'It looks exactly as if the locator blew up and did that damage,' said Marsh. He undid his tie and slumped into a chair. 'Hurry with the coffee.'

Jane sat down.

'I suppose the first detail we ought to look at is how this vanishing trick is carried out,' she said. 'It could be a big help. The girl's body vanished. Hamlet vanished, dead or alive. Hardwick vanished, alive.'

'But in each case there was a simple conjurer's trick to divert your attention at the crucial moment,' Marsh said. 'The camera flash went off: you looked round, half-blinded: Hardwick vanished.

'The milkman cometh. He talketh as milkmen sometimes do from loneliness of the round. He goeth, the body is gone.'

'And in the case of the girl?' Mary asked.

'I deliberately gave them the chance to get her away.'

'But why did you think they would?' Sheila almost shouted.

'The room was bugged,' Marsh said. 'The only reason I could think of was for the murderer to hear what we would do, and it seemed he meant Maureen to be hooked for it. Everything seemed in order for a big scene.

'There was evidence of a row between Maureen and Betsy, Maureen coming here, the shots being stolen, her being a bit tight, going back and probably starting the row again.'

'The row was over a man?' said Sheila.

'What do you think?' said Marsh, watchfully.

'I can't imagine her being interested in anything else,' said Sheila. 'I say! It wasn't about *you*, was it?'

Marsh was startled. Even he hadn't thought of that one.

'Did you stop on the way?' asked Jane coolly.

'A moment only,' said Marsh, shifting in the chair.

'And what happened?' Jane pressed.

'Somebody tossed a tear bomb in on us.'

'You weren't looking at the time?'

'No.' He drank some coffee and stared out of the window.

'You've got an awful lot of that jazzy Irish lipstick on your collar,' Sheila said. 'Who do you think threw the bomb? Her lover?'

'No, I think it was our vanishing artist. Pity I didn't see the car.'

'A great pity,' Jane said.

'Cut the ice,' Marsh said. 'It was a fight, not a flirt. Her seat wasn't fixed.

She fell back, grabbed me. Like that. To save herself.' He shifted again.

'It seems it could have started something,' said Mary. 'But was it you the row was about between her and Betsy?'

'The trouble with you women,' said Marsh, 'is you just cannot see above sex's ugly head. It has to be a triangle, a love set, a Mary Comfort's column. It's got to be boy meets girl. And that's just what was intended. To make everybody think Maureen the nymph was embroiled with another man.

'I didn't. And I gave the impression in that bedroom when the bugging was on.'

'But the row was definitely about someone,' Jane said. 'Mannfred told you so.'

'Yes, but Maureen and Betsy didn't row about a man,' said Marsh. 'It was over a woman.'

* * *

'You must persuade her to take things more easily, Richard,' Dr. Bronson said, closing his bag.

'She wasn't drunk,' said Mannfred. 'I keep telling you she was slipped some raw spirit in a tooth glass.'

'Well, it won't do any harm to take things easily,' Bronson repeated. 'She lives a little wildly, you know.'

'She was perfectly sober the night she slid down the banisters,' said Richard. 'It was a party. Everybody was very happy. Some idiot pushed her off.'

'Yes, I remember you saying so,' Bronson said, dryly. 'What about you? Done nothing about losing some of that excess baggage yet?'

'You're wrong,' Mannfred said. 'I'm having a gym fixed up here under expert management.'

'Really? Who's that?'

'The LOHM Company. A very attractive set-up, very efficient. Know their job.'

'I don't seem to have heard — '
Bronson said, shaking his head.

'They're here now, fixing the gym,' Mannfred said.

'I hope they do you some good,' Bronson said, and went out into the warm morning air.

Mannfred turned when he had gone. Marsh came up behind him, looking at his watch. He continued to look while the doctor drove away from the house.

'He has a transmitter in his little black bag,' Marsh said.

'He? You must be joking!'

'This kicker doesn't joke. Has he been your doctor a long time?'

'A couple of years. He took over a practice in the town.'

Marsh switched subjects.

'Have you explained about Betsy?'

'I just said she went early.' Mannfred shook his head. 'I hate doing it. I'm a bad liar, but what else? Suppose it was just a hoax? Suppose she wasn't dead at all?'

'Is Clarice here?'

'Half-seven every morning. I told you, she lives alone. This is her life here. Yes, she's here. You can always depend on that.'

Marsh switched again.

'There seems to be a wide network of transmitters, most of them doing nothing but mislead us. The doctor had one. There was one round the Vat last night.

They could be planted on people very easily without them knowing it.'

'Some of them must be the real thing,' Mannfred said uneasily.

He started to pace the big hall.

'Is there one on now?' he said, stopping.

'No.'

'What do you think has happened to Betsy?'

'She was killed, taken away, hidden.'

'We must find her. We can't let this go on. It's like a nightmare.'

'Betsy was a spy, shopped and shot by her own group of spoilers. If you think of it like that, it may be easier to have patience. Besides, there is still the danger that your wife might be accused of the murder.'

Mannfred turned away.

'I've been wondering if it's worth going on with this fight.'

'That's what they want you to wonder.'

'Yes, but it hardly seems worth having one's whole life broken up. And that is what will happen. I don't feel we have any power to stop it. The advantage is always with the attacker. He can always get through, because you don't know when or where he's coming. In this case they seem to be here all the time, but when you look, there's nobody there. That's what's getting me down, Marsh. I don't think I can stand it much more!'

Marsh turned towards the open front doorway.

'Have you spoken to your wife about this?' he said.

'My wife has at present a head split like a gong,' Mannfred said angrily. 'Bronson gave her something which almost certainly will send her off to sleep again. She has the biggest hangover since Noah was a ship's captain.'

'You can't drop it now. They have stepped up the whole campaign because you came to us. They're trying to finish us as well now, and if you back out, they'll succeed on both counts.'

'I'm getting past the time when I can worry over someone else's troubles,' said Mannfred. 'I just want to get my wife safely out of here.'

'It's past the time for that,' Marsh said.

'I have the feeling that this has become a little more than a commercial trick. It's become more than a pressure gimmick. It's become a personal grudge.'

Mannfred turned suddenly.

'What do you mean? How can it be a personal grudge?'

'You said you had no relatives at all, I think?'

'I said none that I knew of.'

'There might be one?'

'Anything is possible. But it would be very distant. So distant as to make no matter.'

'If you died, then, there would be no one to take over the recipe?'

'None legally. My wife, of course. I meant in descent.'

'What would happen if you both died?'

Clarice came into the hall, tall, big, smiling confidently. Her hair was grey and rather untidy. She held a file under her arm.

'Mr. Richard, I wonder if you could spare a moment to deal with this? I promised to ring them back at ten o'clock.'

Mannfred grunted, then went with her into another room. As she went, she turned her head and smiled at Marsh. The door closed behind them.

Marsh walked off down the wide corridor to the old ballroom, now to be the gymnasium — if this business ever went on beyond this dismal morning.

The three girls were in there, directing a couple of transport men to where the equipment was to go. The three girls were there because Marsh — and they — had come to the conclusion that it was getting too sticky for one to be left on her own.

The LOHM office was on auto for phone calls. Marsh could get a re-run any time by calling up from the Land-Rover which they had come by.

He looked at his watch. It was still.

The men finished lumping the stuff and went. The kicker in the watch remained inactive.

'Any news?' Jane asked.

'Mannfred's getting near the end of his tether. The attempt to fix his wife did it. He's got scared for her now. He wants to quit.'

'I said he would,' Jane said. 'After all, he'd get out with a fat prize. No one means to steal the business.'

'Which is why I can't see why they've gone so far,' said Sheila. 'Seems nitty to me, going to all this trouble, murder as well. I mean, why?'

'Murder wasn't meant,' said Mary. 'It slipped, that's all.'

'But why go so near?' Sheila demanded. 'I just don't see.'

'You suspected a chemist,' Jane said. 'There was the fire stuff in that bug, then raw spirit, tear gas, and the knockout gas. That must be the connection.'

'It also connects with Royal G. They have to have a chemist, too, to check on the purity of everything before it goes into the mix.'

'Where's he?' Jane said.

'He turns up only for an hour or two each day,' Marsh said. 'Just in case. Nothing has ever gone wrong, but he's a kind of insurance against it.'

He looked at his watch again and added: 'He'll be in about eleven. I plan to see him then.'

The french windows of the room were open looking down on the sunlit lake.

'We've got to find the body of that girl,' Marsh said, grimly. 'That is the essential. If we find her now, we might find the person responsible. In fact, I'm sure that she was snatched in the end because the murderer realised the link to him might show.'

'Is that what you thought when you let him get it out?' Sheila said.

'It's what I felt. Now I definitely think it.'

'Then you think there was something on the body which identified the murderer?' said Jane.

'I think so. Though I saw nothing.'

'It's possible you saw something about her that registered only subconsciously,' Jane said. 'Describe her again. It'll strike all three of us differently. That gives a chance of spotting an unusual detail.'

'Only a chance,' he said. 'Anyhow, she wore a pair of red sandals and a purple cotton dress.'

'Colour blind,' said Sheila.

'Stockings?' Mary asked.

'I don't think so. No, I'm sure. No stockings.'

'What kind of dress?' Sheila said.

'It was a plain sheath dress, like a sack.'

'Zipper somewhere?' Sheila went on. 'Back? Side?'

'Side, now I come to think. I remember wondering why it was necessary when it looked like a sack with a hole in it for the head to go through.'

'Just this plain sheath dress?' Jane said. 'And sandals?'

'Just that.'

'Hair?' Mary asked.

'The hair was that kind of shortish cut, tumbled effect, like a chrysanthemum. It was messed at the back by blood.'

'A necklace?' Sheila pressed. 'Crucifix?'

'No.'

'Ear-rings?' said Sheila.

Marsh suddenly stared.

'Ear-rings!' he cried. 'One ear-ring!'

'One?' said Sheila. 'What do you mean, one?'

'One,' said Marsh firmly. 'I remember seeing her from the door when I came in first. There was a pearl ear-ring on her ear. Clip-on type, smack in the lobe. Then I saw her from over by the window, and her left ear was almost on the carpet but not quite. There was no other ear-ring. I'm sure of that now.'

'And none on the carpet anywhere?' Jane said.

'I would have seen it. I went carefully over that room, in the corners, under the chairs, the bed — There was no ear-ring could have dropped from her when she fell down, shot.'

He looked at his watch again.

'That could be it,' Jane said.

'I'm damned sure it is,' Marsh said. 'I can see it quite clearly now.'

'It could have been shaken off by the shock of the bullet hitting her in the back of the head,' Mary said.

'Which means she wasn't shot in the room at all.'

'She was supposed to be at the switchboard,' Jane said. 'We did establish that the phones were out for a couple of hours before Betsy was found. Which must mean the murderer hung about until she was found.'

'During that time there was fun and games down at the Vat,' Marsh said.

'How many do you think are in this?' Mary said.

'It seems like dozens,' Marsh said, 'but I'd bet there are far less than we think. Someone is having a go at the old invisible man trick, which always seems to quadruple the odds.'

'For the invisible man trick you must have two people,' Jane said. 'One to attract your attention away from what the other is doing.'

'I remember a boy's story I read at school,' Marsh said. 'It was about a ventriloquist who threw his voice behind the enemy to make him turn round. That enabled the schoolboy hero to conk the villain and knock him out.'

'Are you serious?' Jane said.

'Utterly.'

'I've been thinking,' Mary said, 'about this slip-up that turned out to be murder. If the Fear Makers are employed by a commercial firm, however unscrupulous, however crooked, they'd drop them flat after a murder.'

'Which could be why the body was snatched,' said Jane.

'Could be,' Marsh agreed, 'but I feel the main reason was the ear-ring. Somebody would have looked for it sooner or later.'

'It seems to me possible that that set-up with the body and Maureen wasn't a plant for the police at all,' Jane said. 'The murder happened two hours before. The operator then found it could provide a smashing shock for Mannfred, one that might finally shake him out of fighting any more.'

'Which has damned nearly happened,' said Marsh angrily. 'It won't take much more to shake him altogether. He's very near the edge.'

'Pretty cheeky to use your own murder to shock somebody else out of his senses,' Sheila said.

'She wasn't meant to be dead,' said Marsh. 'It was like *Hamlet*. A shock tactic.'

'But she was dead,' said Sheila. 'And still this crummy beast hoicked her about like a stage prop.'

'You make it sound horrible,' Mary said.

'It is horrible, when you think,' Sheila said savagely. 'He shoots a girl in cold blood from the back, then uses her as a dummy to scare somebody else.'

'That's taking a hell of a risk, too,' Jane said. 'The natural thing for a murderer to do is hide it, not parade it around.'

'That's what makes the whole thing like a ribby nightmare,' Sheila said.

'It doesn't fit,' said Jane with sudden firmness. 'It just doesn't fit anywhere. It's upside down, back to front. You can't make any sense of it whichever way you look at it. Not even when you think these Fear Makers are out to create live nightmares. It doesn't even fit then.'

'There is something wrong,' Mary agreed. 'Something like the single ear-ring.'

'I can see only one thing wrong, unless this gink is truly the grandest Guignol of them all,' said Sheila, staring crossly at the floor.

'Well?' Marsh said.

'Why, the bloody fellow didn't know she *was* dead!' Sheila said defiantly.

Marsh stared, and then began to whistle low and very slowly.

7

‘How didn’t he know she was dead?’ Mary asked, blankly. ‘On your own say-so he was carrying her around like a stage prop. How didn’t he know?’

‘He just thought she was out,’ Sheila said. ‘Look you, these rogues have been using a knockout gas, haven’t they? On Janey and the watchman, Bonus. Suppose the thug thought she’d had a smell of that?’

John Marsh went to the window and looked down on the serene surface of the lake.

‘You could be right,’ he said. ‘But the first essential is to find that body and quickly. Mannfred is on the edge of giving up the fight. If he does that, he loses and so do we. It’ll be the end of our little organisation. We just can’t afford to let him back out now.’

‘And how exactly will you stop him?’ Jane Shore asked, coolly. ‘He’s the boss.’

‘We must produce some definite evidence of progress against these — these Fear Makers,’ Marsh said. ‘There is no other way.’

‘That’s going to be tough,’ Jane said. ‘So far it’s been like catching hold of a puff of smoke.’

‘I admit they’re clever,’ Marsh said. ‘But don’t place their genius too high. It’s illusionist’s tricks they’re using. Now you see it — now you don’t. What we have to find is a simple, logical solution to each trick.’

‘One thing to start with,’ Mary said, ‘is that there’s obviously somebody here with us all the time.’

‘Jiminy!’ Sheila said. ‘Why?’

‘Shifting the bodies,’ Mary said. ‘They must have been watching to be sure we weren’t looking when they did the removal jobs.’

‘Which argues there has been one at LOHM and one here,’ Marsh said slowly. ‘I think you have something there, Mary. But there’s just one thing.’

‘This is going to be shuddersome,’ said Sheila uneasily.

'It is,' Marsh said. 'But the fact is these two people — '

'Why do you say two?' Jane interrupted.

'That's the lowest number it can be. There isn't any evidence of more, though it does look like it at times.' Marsh lit a cigarette. 'So fix two to start with.

'These are not invisible men. They are chemists, or one is. Witness: the knockout gas, the use of raw spirit, the gas bomb thrown into my car, and the fire-throwing chemical in the garage bug. Three of these are non-obtainable commercially. Which argues they are dispensing the stuffs themselves.'

'Only one need be a chemist,' Jane said coolly. 'Then say the other one is a professional illusionist.'

Marsh snapped his fingers.

'An excellent thought,' he said. 'And a formidable combo. The chemist could provide trick material for the sleight of hand man to use. Yes, indeed!'

'Hamlet's on the stage,' Sheila said.

There was a thoughtful pause. Down on the lake a barge turned from the Vat landing stage and chugged slowly out on to the water, heading for the canal entrance.

'Hamlet appeared to be dead,' Mary said.

'Hamlet could have acted it,' said Jane.

'Perhaps he had some drug to help,' said Sheila. 'Such as one that would let him lie still and show no pulse. That wouldn't be very difficult. Then he slunk off when you were talking to — listening to the milkman.'

'That's the simplest explanation,' Marsh said. 'Now what about Hardwick? He sat in a chair, asleep. You turned away because of the letting off of the camera flash the other side of the room. You turned back, he was gone.'

'He, too, could have done his own removal job,' Jane said. 'We have no proof he was asleep.'

'Are you accusing my boy-friend?' Sheila said indignantly. 'Why would he be on their side, anyway? He has the job of doing the picture for the Royal G ads.'

'He told a whopper about when he took those pictures,' Mary said. 'He wasn't here last night. It was the night before. Also he was out there in the car when we went out to find the arson man.'

'Well, you've got a sauce, that's what I say,' said Sheila.

'We have to include everybody to start with,' Marsh said. 'Hardwick could have made a genuine mistake. We must take that into account.'

'We did chase another car,' said Sheila. 'He did the driving.'

'That's one to him,' Marsh said.

'But if he didn't remove himself, who did, and where was he?' Jane asked. 'There was no one in the room with us. All windows and doors were fastened, right through the building.'

'Except the front doors,' Mary said.

'But we could see them through the glass door of the lounge,' Jane objected. 'Nobody came in or went out.'

'Somebody did,' said Marsh. 'This is another common denominator. Somebody came in and went out at our place. Somebody did the same thing in the Vat. Now what has our modern building in common with the eighteenth century barn down there?'

It seemed at first sight there could be nothing. The Vat was built of wood and brick filling; LOHM was steel and concrete. The windows at the Vat were old wooden casements; those at LOHM were double-glazed, non-opening. The doors at the Vat were wood and controlled by latches and hefty bolts, in places even crossbars: at LOHM the mortice lock and bolt made every door as safe as it could be.

'Nothing,' said Jane after a while. 'It's chalk and cheese.'

'Except that both must have some property which helps the conjurer,' said Mary.

'Exactly,' said Marsh. 'What?'

'I bet it's something dead obvious,' said Sheila.

'Leave dead out of it,' said Mary uneasily. 'Let's go through the dramatis personæ. Who could be the chemist?'

'There is a chemist here,' said Marsh. 'I told you just now.'

He looked at his watch.

'He should be here by now,' he went

on. 'I'll go and see him.'

He left the ballroom and went across the big hall. Clarice came out of a room on the right, where she had gone with Mannfred some time before.

'Where can I find Mr. Crow?' Marsh asked.

'Mr. Crow?' she said, with a slow smile. 'Why, right out there. He just came in to collect his mail. You'll just catch him.'

She pointed out through the open door. At the bottom of the steps a small man was about to get into an ancient car which looked as untidy as himself.

Marsh hurried out and down the steps.

'Mr. Crow?'

Crow turned, his hand on the car door. He wore pebble glasses which peered out from beneath a shaggy mass of greying hair. His button nose was purple and he was palpably eating his false teeth as he watched Marsh in frowning query. His dirty grey jacket was splashed with the stains of spilt chemicals.

Marsh explained who he was.

'Oh aye,' Crow said. 'It's a right penetrating look, ye have. What is it ye think I must have done, man?'

'Nothing, I hope,' Marsh said and smiled. 'How long have you been with the firm?'

'Thirty-five years,' said Crow. 'I came down fra Dundee that time ago to here, and I haven't moved onywhere since.'

That seemed to let him out by the front door. When a man stays with a firm that long it is unlikely he would turn against it suddenly. It was common knowledge that when takeovers happen, the older members of the staff go out.

'There was trouble down at the Vat last night,' Marsh said. 'Do you know of any way someone could get in and out without the watchmen knowing?'

Crow chewed his teeth a while.

'I have heerd that someone was gettin' in and out, man,' he said, 'but it could be a tale. Just lately some o' the simpler souls down below ha' been talkin' of the old man o' the lake. That's a johnny supposed to come out covered in weeds and haunt the place.'

'I mean a solid person.'

'Well, what way is there? When 'tis all

bolted and barred there's no way in that I know. The windows ha' been fixed a long time now and the floors are good as rocks. I shouldna like to see onybody try the roof, either. 'Tis a long way up and steep as a mountain. No, I know no way.'

'Have you a lab down there? I don't remember seeing one.'

'No. My lab is at home. Down below I use a room and all the gear I need is in a cupboard. 'Tis not a big job, checking. 'Tis so rare onything is wrong. I'm no a blender, ye see. I just check for impurity.'

'It doesn't take long each day?'

'Oh no.'

'What do you use your lab for? Do you have a sideline?'

'Another income, ye mean? No. Mannfred's pay me well, so that I don't stray fra the fold. Now and again I do a little dispensing for Dr. Bronson, if he is pushed. Nominal charge. 'Tis to help only when the town's shut.'

'Thanks, Mr. Crow.'

He nodded and climbed into his old vehicle. Marsh went back into the hall.

The door of Clarice's office was ajar. She came out.

'You caught him?' she said suavely.

'Just. Thank you. I was asking him if he knew any way for someone to get in and out of the Vat without the watchmen knowing.'

She gave a surprised little laugh.

'What an odd thing to ask him!'

'But he's been here such a long time. He might have heard something over the years.'

'But if there was a way anybody knew about, don't you think it would be stopped up?' she said, with a trace of irony.

'I suppose so,' Marsh said. 'But sometimes a person knows a way which is convenient to him, so he says nothing so that it won't be stopped up.'

'That is possible,' she said doubtfully. 'Though I can't imagine why anybody should want a secret way in and out. After all, it is only a workplace, you know.'

'Nevertheless someone is getting in and out,' said Marsh, rather sharply. 'Can you imagine any reason for that?'

'Boys. A prank,' she said.

'In the small hours of the morning?' Marsh challenged.

'Well, no. That does seem unlikely.'

'Have there been any new hands taken on in, say, the last six months?'

'None.'

'Have you heard of any proposal which might mean redundancy amongst the workers?'

'No. Mr. Richard wouldn't hear of that. He believes one of the secrets of a good product is the interest of the workpeople in it. You can't have that if they start to fear the sack.'

'You stay late in the offices here?'

'I do. I live alone, you see. This business is my life. I have no one else.'

He watched her white, slim hand as she fidgeted with a small golden crucifix hanging from a thin chain round her neck. There was a ridge on her ring finger.

'It must be very lonely,' he said.

'It is enough to drive you mad,' she said, with a sudden show of anger. 'Silence, loneliness. It becomes like an enemy, something waiting in the shadows, something waiting to destroy you — '

She recovered herself and flushed slightly, as if ashamed to have shown any emotion.

'I'm sorry,' Marsh said.

'It was silly of me,' she said. 'I am rather overwrought this morning. Mrs. Mannfred ill, and Betsy gone home without leaving any record of phone calls.'

'Perhaps there were none.'

'But there are two recorded about 6 a.m. There is a counter, you know, which works when the phone is answered or a call is made. The time is stamped on the roll, too.'

'You mean that to record a call the phone has to be answered?'

'Yes. She must have answered them, but left no note of them.'

She went to move away.

'Excuse me, I have to see Mr. Richard.'

She went into the room where she had first gone with Mannfred and closed the door. She obviously would not leave Mannfred alone.

Marsh wondered if that had been her idea all along.

Perhaps Mannfred had been her idea of a cure for the maddening loneliness.

And then Mannfred had gone fishing in Ireland . . .

* * *

Mary and Jane left Trance about eleven. Ostensibly they were going back to the office. In fact they went into the town and in the small block of flats where Betsy Burn had lived.

It was one of two over a branch bank. The entrance was at the side, down a narrow alley between the bank and the Post Office. Jane had a questionnaire form clipped to a board.

They went up the stairs to a small vestibule. There were two doors and a window looking at the blank wall of the Post Office. Flat A had been Betsy's.

Jane went to the door and raised a hand to the bell, then stopped. There was a short angular cut in the jamb by the lock, the tell-tale of a celluloid intrusion.

She pointed to it. Mary looked over the railings down the stairwell.

'Try it,' she said.

Jane pushed the door. It resisted a little, then opened.

'Careful,' Jane breathed. 'Just in case anybody's in.'

There was silence in the flat. Complete silence. Not even a clock ticked.

They closed the door behind them. There was a weird feeling of emptiness in the small passageway. Both girls felt it.

The boarded floor had no carpet. There was no picture on the wall.

'I do believe — ' said Mary, and pushed a door open.

The room beyond was empty. The window looked over a playing field and a park beyond that.

'Yes, I felt it,' Mary went on.

There were two rooms, a kitchen and bathroom. All were empty, stripped bare. Here and there were brighter patches on the walls where pictures had hung. The girls came to a halt in the bathroom.

'It still smells of soap and talc,' Jane said. 'She was here only hours ago.'

'Then who did the removal job?' Mary asked. 'There must have been furniture, pots and pans — '

There came a ring at the bell. The girls looked at each other.

'That's sticky!' Mary whispered.

'Hang on,' Jane said.

She went out into the tiny passage and opened the door.

'Telegram for Miss Burn,' the postman said.

She could tell from his look that he had never seen Betsy Burn, for there was no query in his eyes, just an assumption Jane would be the Burn required.

'Thank you,' Jane said, and took it.

'Any answer?' the man said.

Jane ripped the envelope and looked at the form.

'No,' she said. 'Thank you.'

'Ta,' the man said and went downstairs.

As he went Jane saw the door of the adjoining flat close. It must have been open an inch or two. Jane pushed the door to.

'What's the message?' Mary asked.

Jane showed the form.

BURN SIX BANK FLAT A CARNSTEAD
MEET HERON LOUNGE TWO
TRAMPLEASURE.

'Handed in at — what?' said Mary.

'Burnstead. That's Trance's village,' Jane said. 'The nearest one, anyway. Listen, somebody was at the next flat, listening.'

'Who lives there?'

'I don't — What's that? Hissing? The gas?'

'It's the door!' Mary cried. 'Get back!'

She grabbed Jane's arm and pulled her bodily towards the open door of the kitchen. Both girls almost fell into the tiny room.

'It's that ruddy stuff — ' Jane gasped. 'Shut the door! Don't breathe!'

Mary slammed the door. Jane opened a window and leaned out, breathing slow and deeply. Mary joined her at the next window.

'The stuff they gave you?' she said.

'Yes. I'll never forget that fragrance!' Jane said grimly. 'We're in a spot, Mary! Is there a fire escape your way?'

'There's nothing but a drop,' Mary said.

Jane pulled her head in again and listened. There was a silence in the flat, but the faint sound of voices in the bank below could just be heard. A car hooted out in the street, then accelerated away.

She could hear nothing, but she had the feeling someone was in the passage on the other side of the door. Someone with the knockout gas. 'Out!' she whispered.

'Where?' Mary said.

'There's a ledge out there. Have to see if it's strong enough.'

Jane got on the sill and swung her legs out. Mary did the same through the other window. There was a stone band in the brickwork running round the building. It was protruding two inches from the bricks. The only holds offered by the wall were the steel arcs of the window opener guides. It was little enough, but it was better than staying in the room.

The girls got out, and moved gingerly along until they were out of sight of anyone who might come into the kitchen.

Mary could just see in.

Nobody was about below them.

Mary almost squinted in her eagerness to see the kitchen door. Then slowly, it began to open. She became still, tense, almost forgetting her precarious position on the wall.

For if she could see a face at last — the face of one of the Fear Makers, it could mean the beginning of the end for the conspirators.

The door came wider, but nothing showed save the wallpaper of the passage beyond it. Then she saw the fingers of a hand pushing the door.

The girls were still as statues, flattened against the brickwork.

The vague shape of a head showed. Mary stopped breathing altogether, waiting for it to show itself fully.

It did.

It was a pig's head.

Mary froze with horror as if suddenly pitchforked into a nightmare. Then her shocked sight readjusted itself.

It was a gas-mask she looked at not a face at all.

Then suddenly there was a shout from below them.

'What the hell are you two doing up there?'

The gas-mask turned fully to the windows, then backed away. The kitchen door closed again.

Jane looked down. A man was standing in the yard of the bank looking up at them.

'Looking for dry rot,' said Jane, almost calmly.

'In the bricks?' said the man ironically.

'No, seeing if the air bricks are not fouled up,' said Jane. 'There's been a complaint about rot behind the skirtings.'

'Well, damn me,' said the man. 'Why didn't you ask for a ladder?'

'That would be a good idea,' said Mary sweetly. 'Could you get one for us?'

'I'd sooner fetch a policeman,' he said. 'But I'll take your word — till you get down.'

He went off into a shed and came out again with the ladder. Mary was down first, Jane a minute after.

'Did you see the moving men this

morning?' Jane asked.

'Yes. It was the first I knew she was going. She didn't give notice,' the man said. 'Rather queer that. She was paid up to the end of this month, too. Can't understand it.'

'Nor can we,' Jane said. 'She made the appointment with us.'

'Where do you come from?'

'LOHM,' Jane said. 'Business investigators. We understood she wanted some advice, called, found the door open, went in and couldn't get out again.'

'Why not?'

'Because there was a lunatic outside the door in a gas-mask trying to gas us — '

'*What?*' said the man incredulously.

'True,' said Mary. 'Who has the other flat?'

'Miss Watson. She's away most of the time. Secretary for Mannfred's over at Trance. Miss Burn worked there, too. There's something barmy going on here.'

'Hadn't you better go up and look?' Jane suggested.

'I certainly will!' the bank man said. 'You wait here.'

He turned to a door in the yard wall that opened into the Post Office alley.

'No, we'll come, too,' Jane said. 'You go first.'

He hesitated a moment, then said, 'Okay.'

He went through into the alley, in at the flat staircase and up to the top. The door of Flat A was open.

'Try the other one,' Jane said, close behind him.

He rang the B bell.

'Just open the door,' Jane advised.

'And be careful,' Mary advised.

The man tried the door handle and pushed. The door opened. It took him aback. He even retreated a pace.

'Funny,' he said.

He pushed the door wide. The flat was like the other, but furnished.

'Anybody in?' he called.

Behind him Jane sniffed. Once again she caught the faint smell of the knockout gas.

The man stepped into the passageway. The doors of the three rooms were open.

'There's nobody here,' he said, uneasily.

'It might have been somebody hiding up here, waiting a chance to rob your bank,' Mary suggested. 'He definitely wore a gas-mask, and there was a bank hold-up in Walthamstow last week where they used gas and wore masks.'

'Heavens!' he said. 'So there was. I think we'd best call the police!'

'Look first,' Jane said. 'It may just be empty.'

She almost pushed him forward into the first room. It was furnished, simply, cheaply and was empty. They went on to the bedroom.

The door was only partly open and as the bank man came to it he hesitated.

'I can hear somebody breathing,' he whispered. 'I'd better knock.'

'Don't knock,' Jane said very quietly.

She wriggled past him and pushed the door wider. There was a single bed over near the window overlooking the street. A fair-haired girl was asleep in it, her face towards the door. The sound of the sleeper's breathing was unmistakable.

Jane pointed. The bank man looked in,

then withdrew hurriedly and almost shoved the girls back towards the main door.

When they were outside he closed the door firmly.

'I think I understand,' he said. 'Miss Burn has had her stuff moved and Miss Watson — '

'Who's the girl in the bed?' Jane asked, a queer feeling moving in her, a mixture of dread and misgiving.

'That is Miss Burn,' the bank man said. 'Obviously she is using Miss Watson's flat until her new place is ready.'

He mopped his brow as if he had had a close escape from something.

'But what about this mysterious man?' he said. 'Are you sure? I mean, it's very serious — '

'We were pulling your leg,' Mary said.

'There wasn't a man?' He loked mightily relieved.

'No.'

'Then why *were* you up the wall?' he demanded, looking stronger.

'We were testing out a burglar proof idea,' Jane said quickly. 'We investigate, as

I told you, for commercial firms, insurance and so forth. I had the idea that stone course would give someone a chance of breaking in easily. I was wrong.'

'I have heard of LOHM,' confessed the bank man. 'But I didn't realise you were rather — unorthodox.'

'How would you have tested it?' Mary asked sweetly.

'Well — ' The bank man laughed helplessly. 'I don't know. I suppose the same way. But what made you think about this man in a gas-mask? Why that?'

'It was a gimmick to see if we could persuade you to take out more insurance,' Jane said. She laughed. 'Not seriously. We didn't know who you were. You might have been breaking in the back of the bank yourself.'

The bank man eyed them. They could tell from his expression he thought he had come up against a couple of nuts who really didn't know what they were talking about.

Jane brought a card from her pocket. It was an identity card with photograph which was necessary when working in places of commercial secrecy. He looked at it, then smiled.

'I see,' he said. 'No doubt you have reasons. All the same, you mustn't mind my saying it's extremely odd. Extremely.'

He made a brief sign for the girls to go down the stairs ahead of him. In the alley once more he wished them good morning. He stood there until they had left the alley for the main road.

Jane went into the Post Office and rang Marsh at Trance.

'Anyone on the line?' she asked.

'Not according to my instrument.'

She told him about Betsy Burn sleeping in the bed of Clarice's flat.

'What?' he said.

'She was snoring,' Jane said.

'I'll be damned!' he said. 'There must be two of them!'

'There's one point — urgent immediate,' Jane said. 'I'm sure the bank man is ringing the police at this moment.'

'I'm not surprised. You'll have to pick a way round that. What was the wire? Can you read it?'

'I read it there is a pub somewhere

round here called The Heron. The arrangement is to meet in the lounge. Somebody ought to go.'

'Sheila and I have been looking for the corpse. We can call it off now. Haven't seen Mannfred all morning since you went. Clarice has monopolised him.'

'Clarice thought she was going to have him.'

'You think that? It occurred to me.'

'I think that fishing trip to Ireland could be at the root of this whole trouble,' Jane said. 'Like you said, about the row being over a woman, not a man.'

'I think it was over Clarice. Yes.'

'But why bring Betsy in? What had Betsy to do with such an argument? Maureen and Clarice might have resented each other, but where's the outside girl rowing with Maureen over Clarice?'

'A power problem,' Marsh said. 'Are you waiting for something?'

'Sure am,' Jane said. 'I'm waiting for Mary to signal the police have arrived. But they haven't.'

'If they don't come soon,' Marsh said, 'go see the bank man.'

'Right. What to do otherwise? Go back to the office?'

'Yes. Keep a listen out there.'

Jane rang off and went out to where Mary waited on the pavement. They walked along the little shops a while, then turned and walked back. No police showed up.

'We'll see the bank man,' said Jane.

When they got to the bank, it was shut.

'Mondays, Wednesdays, Fridays,' Mary read out, '10 a.m. to 12.'

'So he wasn't even open when he found us,' said Jane. 'Is that odd or not?'

8

Mary and Jane stood on the pavement outside the branch bank.

'So it's been closed over ninety minutes,' Mary said.

'Half an hour before we went into the flat up there,' Jane said. 'In branch banks, you remember, when business ends they just collect everything, take it with them, go out and lock up. Most are clear in ten minutes. There's always a car waiting.'

'We did hear one pull away while we were up there.'

'Then we heard voices in the bank after that,' Jane said.

'Yes.'

They looked at the front of the bank again. The small country town was quiet. It was an early closing day. It looked almost as if most people had gone to bed.

'Then who was the bank man?' Mary said. 'He went back into the yard round the back. I think we might look, even if only to see why he didn't call the police about us.'

They went into the alley at the side of the bank then halted. It was quiet there; no sound of anyone near.

'This wants watching,' Jane said. 'There was that gas slinger up in the flat.'

'There was that girl, too,' Mary said suddenly.

'Why say it like that?'

'Well, we were shooken at the time and didn't see the point, but if that bank man was a genuine bank man, surely he would have wakened her up and asked if everything was all right? After all, he found us wall climbing, then we told him about the gas man.'

'We're a couple of goons,' Jane said. 'Specially after we know the girl was dead and her body snatched. Let's have another look before we bother with the bank.'

They went back into the flat stairway. Jane brought a small pistol from her bag as they came to the landing. The doors of the flats were open, everything was quiet.

'Form a rearguard,' Jane said. 'I'll just look.'

She went into the passage of Flat B, where Betsy Burn had been snoring in her sleep. Mary stayed on the landing, watching the stairs and the other door.

Jane came out.

'She's gone,' she said bitterly. 'There was a tape doing the snoring. It's still doing it. Somebody forgot to switch it off.'

'Then she *was* dead. It was the body John's looking for, and the bank man hogged the doorway, stopped us going in to wake her.'

'After we'd seen her and heard her,' Jane said.

'This is faithful Clarice's flat,' Mary said. 'Let's go back and have a good look round.'

They went in, closed and bolted the door behind them and made a swift survey of the little flat. There was little to see. It was plainly furnished with old furniture, looking like stuff bought about ten years before and not much used.

The bed was ruffled where the body

had been dragged out of it.

'Switch off that tape!' Mary said. 'It gives me the willies, snoring away regardless.'

Jane snicked it off. The silence came like a creeping thing.

'Why the pantomime, anyhow?' Mary asked. 'Why the sleeping beauty arrangement?'

'I think the body was here. When we were found in the next flat they meant to double our intelligence back on itself and show us the girl alive. That was after the gas attack failed and bank man saw us from below.'

'So he had somebody here.'

'Yes, two of them again, as John said. The minimum requirement for an illusionist.'

'Which means quick adjustment of their plans,' Mary said, looking round the room. 'Having failed to get us with gas in the next flat, they swung round and organised a fake set-up to show Betsy Burn was still alive. But if the bank man was in cahoots with the gas man, why did the gas attack get suspended?'

'Something must have happened,' Jane said. 'Something which made it dangerous to carry on with the attack.'

'Well, what?'

'Exactly — what? I don't remember anything happening when we were cliff hanging. Do you?'

'Suddenly bank man was there.'

'And suddenly, gas man backed out. He could have leaned out the window.'

'But we would have crashed to the ground. Was that what he was afraid of?'

'Do you really think he was that considerate?'

'After the murder we tend to lose sight of the fact these Fear Makers are employed by a commercial firm somewhere in the background. Such employers wouldn't condone violence. They might close their eyes to a lot of things, but not that.'

'I'm sure John was right: the girl's death was a trick that went wrong and too far.'

'Yes, but it does leave them with a murder on their hands, which has changed the whole thing from their point of view.'

There was no doubt of that. What had been a commercial pressure game had suddenly slipped into something far worse. In fact, it might have brought the game out of control. Industrial espionage is rife, and normally it is easy for the spy to contact the boss's secretary or someone in control whom he can bribe in one way or another. When the firm is close and loyal, like Mannfred's, a much more militant line of approach is needed, which in itself calls for more secrecy.

Whoever the Fear Makers were, they had clearly got some theatrical ideas about penetration. They had only to indicate continually that penetration was being effected to spread uneasiness in the firm.

Once that was done, the Fifth Column could move in and take control.

The case of Royal G was coming close to that stage. Mannfred wanted to give in. If he did, that would take LOHM into defeat with him.

All this was very clear to the two girls as they stood in the silence of the empty flat.

'The illusionists are working with Clarice,' Jane said, abruptly. 'That must be the connection.'

'Or Betsy was put in the flat next door to keep tabs on Clarice?' Mary suggested. 'It could work that way, too.'

'But John said Maureen and Betsy rowed over a person. He said it was a woman. What other woman has to do with the two? Only Clarice, so far as we know.'

'Could be,' Mary said. 'I think we ought to look into her hiding places. I hate it, but I think we must if there's any doubt.'

She opened one drawer in a chest. Then she took out a photograph and handed it to Jane.

'Wedding scene,' Mary said. 'Clarice, no less. But she is supposed to be a spinster, a ringless wonder. When was this?'

'Judging from the fashions there,' Jane said, 'about ten years ago — '

'That man — the happy groom!' cried Mary. 'You know who that is? Hamlet. The fake dead man on our lawn!'

'It is, too!' Jane said. 'Now there's a line to work on at last. It must be right, as John said, there was an actor in the set-up, a man used to dramatic presentation, and a man who knows how to set a stage for tricks, how to lead an audience's eyes away from what is really happening. A line at last. A firm, solid electric power line. This is going to shock somebody! Put it back. We'll get out of here and back to Trance.'

'Just a minute. You've forgotten the wire — the pub called The Heron. Who sent that? From what you said Betsy's fellow crooks knew she was dead. Why send a wire to her?'

'You would!' Jane snapped. 'Just when we get the apples piled on the cart you go and take a wheel off.'

'But it is true, isn't it?'

'It damn well is. But there's only one way to settle it. That's to keep the appointment.'

'Agreed. But there is one point.

Whoever wired knew she was on last night and off today. So the sender must be in close contact with the firm and her work.'

'We'll soon know.'

They went out to the front door and listened a moment. All was quiet. Mary slid the bolt. Jane held her gun ready. But outside the landing was empty. They went out, down the stairs, into the alley and reached the street. They saw nobody at all until they went down towards the car park. Then it was only a group of youths heading for the playing field with cricket things.

'I remember John said to go back to LOHM,' said Jane.

'After The Heron,' said Mary firmly. 'I want to see this wiring character. I want to be in at the kill.'

'I hope you're right. At least we're sure to meet John. He'll be there.'

* * *

Somewhat earlier, after Jane had rung from the Post Office, John Marsh put down the phone and went back into the ballroom.

Sheila was standing at the french windows, looking out at the lake.

'Don't move,' she said. 'I think that boat's sinking. Either it's sinking or shrinking. Look!'

She pointed. John saw the barge which had left the landing stage a few minutes before. The barrels and crates piled on its deck seemed very close to the waterline. In fact there seemed to be hardly any hull left at all above the surface.

They could hear the chugging of the diesel engine on the still air of the morning.

'Glasses!' John snapped. 'In the bag!'

She darted to the hold-all of 'Gym' equipment which included binoculars, got them out and rushed them to Marsh. He took sight and fixed on the barge.

'There's no one on deck!' he snapped. 'The damn thing's adrift with the motor going! Quick!'

He ran out down through the hall and into the drive. She ran after him, her long legs striding like a man's. They jumped into the LOHM Land-Rover, started off, swung round and tore down along the track through the forest. As they came down near the Vat they could hear shouts and blowing of whistles from the quay.

'They've spotted it now, anyway!' Marsh said.

They swept into the loading yard, went through it, steering between the crate mountains and stopped almost overhanging the water on the loading stage. A dozen men and women were gathered up at the far end, shouting, staring at the barge slowly driving itself on a long, slow course into a watery grave.

Already water was lapping over the sides and barrels were beginning to rock and topple slowly as the water tried to deepen and float them off the deck.

As Marsh and Sheila jumped down to the boards a man shouted: 'You can't do anything! The old cow's going! Someone opened her cocks! For Gor's sake! This is gonna do me, this is!'

Marsh went to the bargee.

'You know the engine's going?'

'So is my beauty!' he groaned.

'How does it start?'

'I got a starter on it. Batt'ry. What am I gonna do? I was just finishin' me tea. Just finishin' me tea!' He wailed as if this information might help him in his distress.

Barrels and crates were beginning to float on the deck. One or two rolled suddenly, cleared the rail and bobbed away on the water. They sank until almost submerged then floated like mines on the smooth water.

'This is the bloody end!' Marsh muttered. 'This is it, Sheila. That's us sinking out there. This will convince Mannfred once for all the fight's no good!'

'Surely you can do something?' she said. 'You can't just stand there!'

'I'm afraid that's all there is to do. There is nothing that can be done about the wreck. There are a couple of men taking a rowing-boat out over there. They'll ship a few barrels — '

'The punt! She'll foul the punt!'

The cry rose up from the stricken bargee as the sinking vessel headed for a still, solitary figure sitting fishing in the punt.

'He's doing nothing! He's just sitting there!' Sheila cried. 'Can't he hear?'

'He's been sitting there for two days,' Marsh said. 'He's always there. Hi! Hi there! Look out!' He added his voice to the rest.

The bellowing and shouting echoed in the trees, rang in the forest and seemed to fill the sky with volume. The man must have been deaf not to have heard it.

Yet he made no move.

As the barge bore down on the light punt the shouting stopped, as if silenced by horror. The barge ploughed into the little craft. They saw it tip over and the man flung out into the lake. The sinking barge thrashed on over the wreckage, shedding floating barrels and boxes in a steady widening path behind it.

'It's going into the bank!' the bargee shouted. 'It'll save her! It'll save the old cow!'

The sudden realisation that there was yet a chance for the love of his life made him forget altogether the tragedy of the solitary fisherman.

The rowing-boat put out. The barge began to rise at the bows, slowing down as it grounded on the sandy bottom. It shoved on a bit, like an open-top whale, heaving itself further from the water, then lurched to a standstill, the water still frothing round the stern where the screw tried fruitlessly to push it on.

There were barrels and crates, cardboard boxes, loose stuff from the deck all floating in the gloomy wake behind the barge, but nothing was seen of the fisherman.

Then amid the floaters there appeared what looked like a table top.

'It's the punt bottom,' Marsh said, hoarsely.

'Where is the man?' Sheila said.

'Let's get looking,' Marsh said, and went back to the truck.

He and Sheila jumped in and backed away, round to the gate again. A man in uniform stared at them from the side of the yard gateway, then suddenly gave a shout.

'Hey, hey! Who are you?' he bawled.

'Stop! I thought you were the Governor!'

Marsh stopped.

'Just trying to save a life,' he said briefly. 'Be back.' He shoved the gear in again. 'Ask the Boss who I am.'

He drove off.

'If that zealous guard's been there all morning,' he said, between his teeth, 'then the saboteur must be one of the workpeople. That's that.'

'It could have been someone hiding on the barge when it came in,' Sheila said.

'If he was he certainly didn't go out with it, and he hasn't got out past that watchdog, I'll bet.'

They sped on along the narrow, bumpy track round the lakeside. This road was used only by fishermen and Mannfred himself for walks and relaxation.

They ran along it until the shape of the barge wreck showed down between the trees. Marsh stopped. They got out and ran down the soft pine-needled slope between the tall trees. At the water's edge they stopped and looked out at the dismal scattering of debris.

'There's a line there,' Sheila said.

'Look! It goes out to the punt.'

Marsh looked to where a line had been spiked into the ground near the edge of the small, overhanging bank. It vanished into the water but the overturned punt showed the other end of it, fifteen yards out on the lake.

'He didn't struggle and he didn't float,' Marsh said, scanning the water. 'Where is he? A live man couldn't sink like a stone.'

The barge engine had stopped. Across the lake the sound of the voices on the landing stage seemed distant, almost remote. The plash of the rowing-boat oars came nearer over the silent surface of the water.

Marsh waded into the water and got a grip on the bows of the barge. He hoisted himself up and on to the tilted deck, now almost clear of cargo. He went down the sloping planks looking down over the side. The water had settled after the stirring of the boat screw, and small fish darted in the clear water as if eager to examine the new arrival, a wooden whale.

Then further off, near where the punt drifted and dragged its line, Marsh saw a dark shadow down under the surface of the water. It wavered, shrank and swelled with the quiet movement of the lake, but it was recognisable.

It was a man's body, spreadeagled on the sandy bottom.

Marsh threw his jacket on the deck and dived shallowly into the water. He did not surface again but went in a flat dive down to where the man lay.

The only moving things about him were his clothes, wavering uneasily with the water currents. Small fish scattered, darting away like streaks of coloured light. The weeds put out curious, stroking fingers towards the swimmer.

Marsh got an arm round the shoulder of the body. It was hard, unyielding.

He let a small stream of bubbles burst upwards, then gripped a shoulder of the body and heaved it over. Sand rose and drifted like small depth charges dissipating in the sunlit water.

Marsh stared down on the gross, distorted face of a monster, shiny, garish, blank and dead, as the black soft hat fell back to show the features of a ghoul.

Marsh felt a horror, a sickening revulsion.

The shadow of the rowing boat came silently overhead.

A moment later a line dropped down to him. He was in good training. His breath would last a little while longer. He took the line, snatching at the drifting, twisting snake, then looped it round one of the body's ankles and pulled the line in signal.

The men in the boat began to haul. The body's leg raised and the lower half of the body began to follow it upwards.

Suddenly the foot came right off and drifted away, falling slowly. The body dropped back, cushioned by the water and a great burst of sand surrounded it and fogged the view.

Marsh swam up to the surface and breathed hard.

'It broke,' a man said. 'You all right?'

'Give me the line again,' Marsh said.

He took it, doubled over, then dived down to the body once more. This time he got the rope under the arms and round the chest. Then he surfaced once more.

'Haul away,' he gasped, treading water.

'It weighs a ton!'

The men began to pull.

'Crimey!' one panted. 'What is he? Ten-ton Ted?'

They rested a while then went on pulling. The awful face came out, running water, its gruesome colours painted bright in the sun, water running out of the gaping mouth.

Sheila screamed from the bank and covered her face with her hands.

Marsh swam up and gave the two men a hand to get the angler over the side and into the boat. He landed in the bottom like a fall of rocks.

'What the hell's that?' one boatman said.

'A lonely fisherman who never caught anything but a lot of prize mugs like me. Gentlemen, let me introduce Lord Bug of Trance!'

They thought he had swallowed too much water.

So Marsh was not at The Heron at the appointed time.

* * *

The Heron was a large inn on the main road out of town. The car park ran all round it, painted into parking sections, but there were only four cars scattered widely out, when the girls drove into it.

'Quiet day in Dodge City,' Mary said. 'I hope it isn't cleared out for a shooting match.'

'Anything could happen,' Jane said, 'except that according to our book, whoever we're going to meet doesn't know Betsy is dead.'

'I'm betting on nothing,' Mary said.

They walked towards the door marked lounge. Through the window beside it they could see a long, orange lit bar with a barmaid polishing glasses behind it.

'Looks empty,' Jane said.

Mary pushed the door and went in. There was no customer in the bar at first sight, but when they got to the counter they looked round and saw a large bow window with a settee, tables and chairs in it. A man and a woman, apart, it seemed, sat with their backs to the window, looking out over the river beyond the rear car park.

It was then ten to two.

Jane ordered two Martinis. The barmaid watched them with faint curiosity through the mirror at the bar back as she got the drinks, but her face was blank when she turned round with them.

They sat on stools.

'It's quiet, isn't it?' Jane asked.

'Always is, early closing.' The barmaid looked at the clock. 'It's getting on a bit, too. We get plenty up till half one and some later.'

A waiter came in from another bar and she went to talk with him. Mary watched the two at the bay window, but the man, shoulders hunched, shining bald head tipped forward, could have been asleep. The woman, grey-haired and rather tweedy, was reading a magazine. They came under suspicion though the girls would be disappointed if either turned out to be the mysterious Trampleasure.

'It's a falsie, that name,' Mary said. 'Somebody got it out of a phone book, I'll bet.'

The hands of the clock crawled on.

'Where's John, anyway? And Sheila?' Mary looked at the clock for the second time in a minute.

'Something cropped up, perhaps,' Jane said.

'Two o'clock,' Mary said, almost casually. 'Nobody present like Trampleasure. Two what day, I wonder? It didn't say. I'm itchy. Can't keep still.'

The clock crawled on. The barmaid polished more glasses. The tweedy woman changed her magazine for another from the inn stock. The bald-headed man moved, looked at his watch, took a drink and settled down again.

'I'll take a sandwich,' Mary said. 'I'd forgotten my smallest Mary.'

The barmaid came and went out through a service door. She came back with nothing.

'The waiter'll bring it,' she said.

A couple of minutes went by before the waiter came in, making an elaborate fuss with a few small-cut sandwiches on a tray. He was big, had sideboards, black hair and horn-rimmed glasses. He smiled, dusted the counter and finally set the small plate down.

'Five shillings, madam,' he said, beaming at the outrageous price he asked.

She paid and he went away out of the lounge again. Mary began to eat.

Quarter past two.

At eighteen minutes past, Richard Mannfred came in. He came straight to the bar and then saw the girls.

'Why, hallo,' he said. 'What's this? A rest from weary labours? Lottie, fix me some sandwiches, will you? Ham. And a large Scotch. Will you join me, ladies?'

He was very cheerful, fat and filled with *bonhomie*. He monopolised them. If Trampleasure arrived finally, they would hardly get a chance to identify him with Mannfred bouncing about with this overdone cheer.

'We're not actually just relaxing,' Jane said quietly. 'We're waiting for someone.'

'Anyone I know?' Mannfred said, becoming grave.

'Do you know anyone called Trampleasure?' Mary asked.

'Yes. The waiter's name is Trampleasure.'

Mary stiffened. Jane stared at the sandwiches.

'The waiter!' Mary said.

'He'll be coming in with the sandwiches,' Mannfred said. 'Why?'

'It doesn't matter,' Jane said. 'Have you been with Mr. Marsh this morning? He should have been here now.'

'No, I haven't seen him since early this morning. It's been a heavy day. A considerable amount of work which I left over from yesterday, with all the excitement going on then.'

'You don't know if anything happened that could have held him up?' Mary asked.

'I really wouldn't know,' Mannfred said. 'I've been working in my office up at the house with my secretary all morning. There was a very considerable amount to be done.'

'Did you trace the overnight phone calls?' Jane asked. 'Mr. Marsh said there was some confusion about them.'

'We settled pretty well everything,' Mannfred said. 'At least, if anything remains unsettled it will stay so, I assure you.'

He laughed.

'We saw Miss Burn this morning,' Jane said.

'My God!' Mannfred said. 'Where? You found her, you mean?'

'We saw her,' Jane said. 'She was in your secretary's flat. So somebody got her away from the house last night, although you didn't hear any vehicle go off.'

'She wasn't very big,' Mannfred said. 'A fair-sized man could have carried her. A car could have been waiting a way off. I don't think that point is important. I told Mr. Marsh so.' He looked round at the clock. 'Where's the damned man with my sandwiches?'

'How is Mrs. Mannfred?' Mary asked.

'Fair, fair,' he said. 'She has the equivalent of a seven-day hangover. Have you ever sampled the joys of pure spirit? I can assure you it is like skimming the top off melted boot polish. Where is that man? Lottie! I don't want to be here all day. You'll be shutting in a minute.'

'I'll jolly them along,' Lottie said.

She went to the house phone and said: 'What about those ham sandwiches? Are you curing the ham? Oh, I see. I'll lock up, then. That'll be all right.'

She rang off and came back through the flap in the counter, raising it like a drawbridge.

'I'll lock the doors and then you needn't bother. Nobody else'll get in and you can eat in your own time. Finish your drink, though.'

'Very kind of you,' Mannfred said.

The girl went and locked the lounge door, then came back behind the bar. The waiter came twirling in through the swing service door like a dancer, bearing another tray.

He came up with it.

'Is your name Trampleasure?' Jane asked.

'You're joking, of course,' the waiter said, pointing to Mannfred. 'That is Mr. Trampleasure.'

Said a voice behind the girls: 'I am Mr. J. T. Trampleasure.'

They looked round, staring into the face of the baldheaded man. The tweedy woman stood to one side of him, beaming.

'I am Miss Trampleasure,' she said. 'No relation.'

'I am the other Miss Trampleasure,' said Lottie. 'No relation, either.'

Quite suddenly the two girls found themselves surrounded by Trampleasures, all of whom smiled in an unpleasant way.

'Of course,' said Mannfred. 'You know I'm not one.'

The waiter put the tray down on the counter and lifted the lid off the dish.

There was a revolver underneath.

9

John Marsh had spare shirt and slacks in the Land-Rover. There were always some in there, meant rather for the possibility of drenching rain than diving for dummies in Trance Lake.

Sheila stood beside the truck while he changed within.

'A horrid-looking thing,' she said.

'It depends if you like waxworks,' he said. 'They frighten me stiff, for some reason. Perhaps I was scared by a doll when young.'

'Yes, but why? Why the angling act, I mean?'

'The gentleman was full of transmitters,' John Marsh said. 'He was the source of the intermittent signals my detector picked up. They were beamed from his belly to the Vat, and up to the house by clockwork control.'

'So there never was anybody listening in?'

'Oh yes, there was.'

He jumped over the tailboard to the ground. Through the trees on the slope down to the water the half-sunken barge lurched. The rowing-boat, carrying the dummy, was making a slow way back across the smooth water to the landing stage.

'The waxwork was a decoy,' Marsh said. 'It's very odd how people get used to seeing something so often they soon cease to see it at all. If it wasn't for that trait in the human view, that robot would have been investigated before.'

'And so there is somebody still listening?'

'And sinking barges and fouling good drink and doing disappearing tricks and murders,' he said. 'Come on. Back to the Vat. I want to speak to the guardian of the premises.'

'What about the girls? That telegram type message they had?'

He looked at his watch.

'It's too late to make that pub now,' he said. 'Perhaps they'll go and keep an eye on Trampleasure. If not, we'll have to let it ride. It could have been a decoy, too. Decoys are a feature of the case, distracting the attention to an innocent spot while the deed is done elsewhere.'

'Suppose it isn't?'

'It's too late for us to find out,' he said. 'Let's go.'

She got in. He swung round amongst the trees and bumped on to the track again. They came into the Vat yard and stopped. Even as they did so, the uniformed yardman held up his hand for the truck to stop.

Clearly, his having already mistaken the vehicle for Richard Mannfred's, he was not going to err again, even if it meant stopping the Boss just to make sure.

Marsh got out.

'Did you admit any strangers today? Anyone at all? Lorry drivers, messengers? Anything, anybody?'

'No strangers, no,' said the yardman. 'When I got here there was just Bonus and Jass. They hadn't let in anybody. We're all pretty sharp now. Everything is going funny. Nobody likes it much.'

'You know the master of the barge?' Marsh asked.

'Aye. He comes regular.'

'What time did he get here?' Sheila asked.

' 'Fore I come on that was. Usually he gets here round eight, but it was early this morning. Fine mystery that is. Sinkin' like that.'

'What about it sailing away on its own?' said Marsh.

'Somebody must of untied her — '

'And started the engine?'

'Well, no. That's funny. Somebody must of bin aboard. I hadn't thought of that. But it weren't Terry, for he was drinkin' tea with his master when she slipped out on the water.'

'And nobody else was here you didn't know well?'

'I know everybody that works here. That's my job.'

'Most of them come in a bus?'

'Some has cars, too. They uses the cars payday and a bit after and comes in the free bus after that till payday again.'

'What about Jass and Bonus?'

'They got a ten-pound banger they uses. Company pays the petrol.'

'Let's have another look at the landing stage,' Marsh said.

The yardman came through the gate with them and closed it behind him. Clearly he was very nervous about all the inexplicable things that were going on around him.

The barge master and his mate, Terry, had borrowed a dinghy and gone across to the wreck. The floating barrels still dotted the water of the lake, but most of the cases had sunk.

The landing stage was built out from the shore on foot-square piles driven into the sand bottom. Any small boat could sail in under the boards of the stage itself.

A vehicle came into the yard, and the yardman turned quickly and hurried away to see who it was. The rest of the workpeople had gone into the Vat. The stage was empty.

'Like I said, somebody in the firm has been got at,' Marsh said. 'It's perfectly obvious now that this is an inside job inspired from outside.'

'Well, if I had to guess anybody I'd guess two women; Clarice and Maureen,' said Sheila.

'But Clarice is jealous of Maureen. She monopolises Mannfred as if she gets some pleasure in hogging him from his own wife.'

'Why does he let her? He doesn't seem a weakie.'

'Mannfred could be slightly schizo. Sometimes he's firm and determined, at others he goes slack and wants to give up.'

'Well, he's certainly left us a clear field this morning,' Sheila said. 'I haven't seen him since ten. It's after two now.'

Marsh sat on a bollard and stared out over the lake towards the house on the hilltop.

'Let's think again,' he said. 'Maureen. She could have put Jane out in the changing-room. Her car was outside, and she wasn't in it. But she was with me when Hardwick vanished. She was flat out when Hamlet was found on the lawn.'

'But not when the girl was killed,' Sheila said.

'We don't know that. The picture forming in my mind is that Maureen is very simple and uninhibited and easily fooled, yet for some reason the Fear Makers want to keep her quiet. How could a simple, uninhibited, rather silly woman be of danger to clever men like these? What are they afraid she might see through?'

'Men,' said Sheila. 'If it's to do with Maureen it must be men. She isn't interested in anything else.'

'A harsh cut, but could be right,' he said slowly. 'But what men?'

'Her husband doesn't satisfy her, does he? If he did, she wouldn't chase the rest. She's a hot lady. She needs affection, so my guess is Mannfred doesn't give her any.'

'Well, what happened on the fishing trip in Ireland?' Marsh said. 'I said before and I still think that something began there which caused all this.'

'Something to do with Maureen's nature,' Sheila said firmly. 'Passionate, affectionate, carefree — a knockover for Mannfred — but only if he returned some of her own heat. You get me, Sherlock?'

'You musn't judge him as of now. He has been worried for some time and that takes a man's mind off love affairs.'

'I need fodder,' she said, turning towards the gate. 'I'm for the sealed sandwiches.'

He got up and followed her out into the yard. There was a lorry there, picking up empty crates, a man whistling loudly as he slung them over the tailboard.

Marsh and Sheila got into the back of the truck. She opened a picnic case, for it had been thought that the signs that day had indicated a possible need for a standby meal.

'What time is it?' she said, handing him a sandwich.

'Three-fifteen,' he said. 'We must have talked a long time — Hallo! A bug! Look at the kicker.'

'I thought all the bugs had been drowned,' she said.

'Clearly not,' he said. 'Let's try the locator.'

He opened a steel cupboard fitted

behind the front seats and the controls of what looked like a television set showed.

'So far this one hasn't got the range of any of the bugs they were using,' he said. 'They seemed to be using a sort of self-jamming signal — '

'What's the matter?'

'It's giving a bearing of three-forty at eleven hundred yards,' he said tersely. 'That means the signal's coming from the house up there!'

'What's so odd?'

'It's Jane's alarm signal from the bleeper in her cigarette lighter!' he said.

'But they're back at LOHM, or — '

'Signal's stopped,' he snapped. 'Now what? Something's happened, Sheila. They're up at the house, obviously in a bad state. That transmitter, you remember, is an absolutely last resort S.O.S. Jane must be in some considerable danger to use that thing.'

'We'd better rush up there!'

'We'd better think a minute. If they are there, and in danger, then we've proved beyond all doubt it's an inside job. But that doesn't make it any easier to deal with. Who is the insider? I think you're right about Clarice, but who else? We must cater for any number. Two is the minimum, but it's probably more. We must suppose they've been collared somehow. Perhaps the pub was a trap.'

'But they're back here!'

'Yes. Which means there are only two of us effectively left, so we must consider ourselves outnumbered. The answer to that is cunning. We'll go back and pretend we have no idea anything is wrong with Mary and Jane and don't know where they are.'

'I'll be sick,' she said.

They clambered over into the front seats and drove back up the hill to Trance. The usual small collection of cars stood in front of the house. Marsh did not see any change in the assortment since he had last seen it.

As they pulled up Sheila saw Clarice standing at one of the open windows on the ground floor, big glasses on, apparently reading through some papers she held in her hand. She did not look up.

As the two went into the hall Maureen

was coming down the stairs. She stopped dead as she saw Marsh.

Marsh halted and said: 'I hope you're feeling better.'

She moved again, and smiled wanly.

'You're kidding, of course,' she said. 'I have a head like a floating mine.' She came on down the stairs. 'I want to talk.'

'Come in the ballroom,' Marsh said. 'That's my temporary office.'

She laughed huskily. It seemed to pain her and she stopped. They went into the ballroom. Marsh looked at his watch. The tell-tale kicker was still.

Marsh closed the door and glanced over at the open french windows. No one was there.

'What's worrying you?' Sheila said, tersely.

'I shot a girl last night,' Maureen said.

Sheila looked quickly at Marsh. Marsh appeared unmoved.

'Why?' he said.

'She made love with my husband.'

Marsh's eyes opened in surprise.

'Betsy Burn?' he said.

'Yes.'

‘Tell me how you know.’

‘I got back here with him. He sent me to my room. He said he wouldn’t have anything to do with me, he was very angry. Kept his back on me. I was upset, but I was wild, too. So I went up. I stayed a while and drank a little Irish whiskey. Then I thought I would make it up and went to his bedroom — the one he uses if he is working late and don’t want to disturb me. They are making love on the bed there — she and him. I got wild. I got mad. I went back to my room. I have a gun he gave me. It is always empty. I thought I would frighten them both, you see? I went back to the room. He had gone downstairs again. She was tidying herself. I pointed the gun and I said, ‘You leave my husband alone or I’ll kill you!’ She laughed and tried to get by me to go out. I said, ‘I will shoot you!’ She laughed in my face as she went by.

‘I pulled the trigger. Nothing was supposed to happen, but there was a shell in it! My God! I stood there and watched her fall on the floor. I was sick. All the wild had gone. I went to the bedside.

There was a glass of water. I drank some. It was damn firewater. I just fell on the bed, dead out.

'This morning I said to Richard, 'I shot the girl'. He said, 'You're dreaming. There's no body here'. The doc came. He gave me a sedative. I slept since. But then I thought, 'John! I shall tell John!' So I am telling you.'

She stopped, her hands writhing together.

Marsh kept looking at his watch. No tell-tale.

'Don't say this to anybody,' he said shortly.

'I wasn't dreaming. It happened. If he had not kept his back to me, and then — on the bed — that girl! I just couldn't help it! I meant to frighten her out of the house. Somebody loaded the gun!'

'Was Richard very cold to you lately?'

'Worried, yes. But he wasn't like the cold you get when there's another woman. Not like that at all. He's always been warm towards me even when he was worried, but suddenly he goes hard. I don't get it. I don't understand what I did. You have to do somethin' to get your man into another girl's arms.'

'But you were trying to make him jealous, too.'

'With you? Oh no. I'm the affectionate kind. I can't help it. That's my kind. It just happens. He understands that. Ye have to understand that, to get anywhere in workin' this out.'

'Work it out!' Marsh said angrily. 'That's going to be easy! You admitting you killed that girl makes everything I've worked out up to now a bag of old nails — worthless! Why did you have to say anything?'

* * *

Maureen looked as if she would cry, but recovered. Marsh walked to the windows, out on to the terrace which was empty. He looked up at the house above him, then turned and went back into the ballroom.

'How many people have you seen come into the house today?' he asked.

'People?' Maureen was surprised. 'But

there are always a number of people. This is a business house, you know.'

'Clarice seems to be very busy today. Is she always?'

'She is always busy to keep near my husband. She's a jealous cow. I would like to — '

The door opened behind her. Clarice appeared there, a notebook clutched to her bosom.

'Oh, I'm so sorry,' she said, and smiled. 'I thought the room was empty.'

'You knew it was occupied,' Marsh said, striding up to her so that she withdrew a pace in surprise. 'You are spying, as usual. As it happens this time it is convenient. What time did Miss Shore and Miss Adur arrive here *this afternoon*?'

The woman flinched, it was a momentary loss of control. She smiled again.

'To my knowledge they went out this morning and have not returned.'

'You are a liar, Mrs. Gaunt,' Marsh said. 'Sit down!'

She started violently. For the first time the ready smile was completely lost. She let Sheila take her arm and sit her in a chair almost before she realised what was happening.

'How did you know? I thought nobody knew. I thought it was all forgotten!' She appeared distrait.

'How can it be forgotten when your husband is continually in contact with you?' Marsh said.

'You don't know what you're talking about!' Clarice burnt up suddenly. 'I'll have you thrown out of the house!'

'How?' Marsh cut in fast. 'Are you the chief here?'

She hesitated.

'Are you?' he said. 'Tell me now! If you find it so easy to assume command, tell me what you are!'

She changed again.

'I didn't think. I'm sorry. I'm overwrought. All this business — '

'Betsy Burn was found dead in your flat this morning,' Marsh said.

'Oh no, no! He wouldn't — ' She almost bit her tongue.

'Who wouldn't? Marsh snapped. 'Explain what she was doing there.'

‘I can’t.’ She controlled herself suddenly, her mouth set hard and firm. ‘I don’t know.’

‘Last night your husband broke into my office and stole rounds of ammunition which would fit Mrs. Mannfred’s gun,’ Marsh said. ‘You know Mrs. Mannfred’s gun, don’t you?’

‘She had a little pistol, yes, but I — ’

‘You told your husband the calibre,’ Marsh said. ‘He stole the ammunition. I might remind you, Mrs. Gaunt, that Betsy’s body is bound to turn up sooner or later.’

‘I think you are mistaken somehow, somewhere — ’

‘When did you telephone and make arrangements for her furniture to be removed from her flat? When? Just when is all I want to know.’

‘She asked me to. She said yesterday. I phoned this morning.’

‘Very early this morning. The place was cleared out by noon.’

‘There was not much there.’

‘It was part of a game, so that people would think she had gone, taking her things with her and wouldn't assume anything worse? The furniture would be gone, she would be gone, there would be your word as secretary that all was above board. She owed nothing. Nobody would ask questions. She had gone, her furniture put into store. All the sudden impulse of a discontented girl.'

Clarice said nothing now. The first shock was over. She appeared to stone-wall until she could see a way to fight back. She found it suddenly.

'Mr. Marsh, I did not want to say this, but you force me. What I did, I did for Mr. Mannfred, to avoid scandal, to avoid this firm being ruined by a sordid tragedy that would have destroyed his position in this difficult industry.'

'You did that for him after you had engineered a murder?'

'I did nothing of the sort! That is your fantastic guess-work! Mrs. Mannfred shot the girl through jealousy! That is the truth of it. She will tell you so herself!'

'Here we go again!' Sheila groaned aloud. 'It keeps coming round to Mrs. Mannfred. But if you did that for Mr.

Mannfred, Mrs. Gaunt, weren't you rather fond of him, too? Hadn't you stored up as much jealousy over this girl?'

'I am past the stage for violent passion,' Clarice said, and sneered. 'I don't think any man worth a life in prison.'

'Yet you risked it in trying to cover the murder,' said Marsh. 'What's the difference? You'll risk it cold-bloodedly but not in the heat of the moment? Is that what you mean?'

'Mr. Marsh, if there was a murder, I wasn't here at the time. I still have no evidence that there was one, and it seems from what you say, nor have you.'

'It will appear,' he said. 'That's what I keep telling you, Mrs. Gaunt.'

'Then I shall wait until I have evidence of it!' She was furiously angry now.

He twisted suddenly and got in under her guard.

'What time did you get back from The Heron? About an hour ago?'

'No — ' She barely uttered the word before she realised the slip. 'The Heron? What do you mean?'

Marsh laughed shortly and turned away.

'Perhaps you went just to meet your husband, having wired him at Betsy's flat,' Marsh said. 'The wire was sent from the town itself.'

'I was with Mr. Mannfred all morning,' Clarice said.

'You sound a little triumphant there,' Marsh said quickly. 'I saw you go in there with him, in the office overlooking the lake. Does he always use that one?'

'Always.'

'And you were there with him all the morning.'

'I have just told you that.'

'It's been a hot day. You had the windows open?'

'Mr. Richard likes the windows open in good weather. There is no air conditioning in the house, only down at the Vat.'

'So you could see and hear what went on outside the lake?'

'I don't understand.'

'Let me put it like this. Around noon you were in town — not in the office. You sent the wire from there.'

'Why should I do such a thing? I live in the next flat!'

'But you couldn't risk being seen going back there until you were sure that body had gone. You wired him to meet you at The Heron at two so you could find out what had happened and be certain the awful thing had been got rid of.'

'Why should I bother about a corpse I didn't kill? She's the one who should worry, not me.'

Marsh turned to Maureen.

'You rowed with Betsy in the bedroom, as you said. You said she passed you to go out of the room. Where was she then?'

'Beyond the foot of the bed, I was. She went to go by,' Maureen said. 'I told her to stop or I'd blow her brains out. She laughed at me, so I — I fired the little gun.'

'How do you know she laughed at you?'

'She laughed in me face!'

'And you shot her then?'

'Yes. I couldn't hold it back any longer!'

'You didn't see the shot hit her?'

'Be jasus no! I shut me eyes when I pulled the trigger. I didn't know what would happen. I never fired a gun before, and even if it's empty, I felt the shivers just the same.'

'When you opened your eyes she'd fallen down?'

Maureen did not speak, but just nodded and turned away. Marsh turned to Clarice again.

'There's your admission,' Clarice said.

'Just one point,' Marsh said. 'Was Betsy the type of idiot child who would turn her back on a wild angry Irishwoman with a gun who was threatening to pull the trigger?'

'She knew they were — ' Clarice had gone too far at last.

'Blanks?' Marsh suggested.

'I know nothing of that!' the woman cried out. 'But she must have turned her back, mustn't she?'

'Must she? But how did you know she was shot in the back of the head? You didn't see her dead, you say. The only other way you could have known is — '

'Richard told me!'

'Richard Mannfred told you his wife had shot a girl in the back of the head and that the body had disappeared?' Marsh laughed again. 'Do you really ask me to believe Mr. Mannfred is that stupid? What possible reason could he have had? Just give me one that I may be swayed.'

'He tells me everything.'

'To do with business. Give me a reason, or just tell me when he told you this.'

'This morning, in the office.'

'You were there with him all the time until you went off into town about noon?'

'I did not go into town! I was there in the office with him until lunch-time — after.'

'Why didn't you and he run out when you saw the barge kill the fisherman?'

There was a weird silence. Clarice swallowed.

'Kill the fisherman?' she croaked.

'How was it that you, with the windows open, didn't hear all that shouting and the whistles when the barge ran him down?' He waited a moment. 'The answer is simple. You just weren't there. You couldn't possibly have been, could you?'

Clarice sat staring ahead as if she saw a ghost there. 'It couldn't have killed the fisherman,' she said, blankly.

'Why? Wasn't he real?'

At this point, Clarice burst into tears. The hard façade crumbled. She was no longer the efficient woman in charge, but an inefficient woman in the charge of someone else.

Maureen went to her.

'Don't take on like that,' she said gently.

Clarice suddenly reached out and pushed her away.

'Get back, you tart!' she said, furiously. 'None of this would have happened but for you!' Then she bit back more words and mopped the tears from her cheeks.

'Why did it happen?' Marsh asked quietly.

Clarice turned and looked at him again.

'He went to Ireland,' she said. 'And everything was different after that.'

'But why?'

She turned and looked straight ahead,

her lips shut tight together.

'Where are my assistants?' Marsh said.

Clarice started.

'I don't know anything about — '

'You're forgetting now what you've said already,' he said. 'Haven't you?'

The woman was visibly shaken now. The way Marsh kept switching subjects had bewildered her. She had been in a worked-up state to begin with, now she seemed completely confused, unable to remember what she had said.

'I haven't seen them!' she cried out.

'But you said you had,' Marsh pressed. 'Remember? You went to The Heron, met them there and brought them back here with your husband. You said that, didn't you?'

Her eyes went big.

'My God, no! I didn't! I never said that!'

'Why wouldn't you have said it? Because it's the truth?'

She got up.

'This is absurd. I'll stay no longer. I have to be with Mr. Mannfred at four. I must go!'

She went towards the door. Sheila glanced at Marsh. He shook his head.

'Mr. Mannfred,' Marsh said quietly. 'Are you sure you mean Mr. Mannfred?'

She stopped and turned back, her eyes momentarily very big.

'What do you mean?'

'I mean that you haven't seen Mr. Mannfred at any time today,' said Marsh.

'You must be mad! You saw me go into the office with him this morning!'

'I didn't,' Marsh said.

'But we — ' Sheila began.

'Where are my assistants?' Marsh said.

The woman went suddenly slack, then came away from the door, back towards her tormentor.

10

Clarice stood a moment, staring out of the windows.

'You shot Betsy!' Maureen cried out suddenly.

It seemed no more than a flash of Irish intuition, for Maureen stood breathing hard after it as if frightened of what the result might be. Clarice turned and looked at her.

'Yes,' she said.

Sheila let go a hissing breath.

'What's happened that you admit it now?' she said.

'There comes a time when one feels it not worth while to let the strain go on, when you are so tired you must let go.'

She turned, found a chair and sat in it. She looked tired and grey.

'I have a special regard for Richard Mannfred,' she said. 'I came here, years ago with the intention of getting into Mannfred's good graces. Of making myself indispensable to him, and in the end getting hold of the secret on which the wealth of the company is based. That was my intention. Unfortunately it had a boomerang effect. My regard for Mannfred grew until it became almost unbearable.

'I pleaded with my husband for a divorce. He refused. He was determined I should carry out my job.'

'Your husband was in it from the start?' Marsh asked.

'It was his idea. To his odd mind he thought a Bachelor Prince of Booze was an easy target.' She smiled bitterly.

'He was prepared to wait?' Marsh said.

'Certainly. He had his career as an actor. He was looking to the future. He can be a very patient man. Where the trouble began was when I found myself involved with Richard. Gaunt threatened all sorts of things then, not from jealousy, but because he feared for his plan.

'Then Richard went to Ireland and married — this woman. That set me back on the road with my husband. He was delighted. Through his country-wide travels he had got himself in with a man who directed some kind of industrial spy office. He posed as a commercial photographer — '

'Hardwick?' Marsh said.

'Curses!' Sheila hissed. 'I felt I was wrong all along!'

'Yes.'

'I'm letting you go on,' Marsh said, 'because I believe that while you talk my partners will be safe.' He looked at his watch.

'They are with my husband,' Clarice said.

'Where?'

'I don't know. Somewhere in the house. It's very big. There are fifty rooms, many of them with connecting doors. But you are right. He won't do anything until he knows — what has happened to me.'

'Where is Mannfred?' Marsh said.

Both Sheila and Maureen stared in surprise at the question.

Clarice shook her head. 'There are fifty rooms.'

'More vanishing tricks,' said Marsh. 'I have just found what the Vat and my building have in common. Air conditioning. Ventilating trunks connect every room in both places. I never thought of that. An easy way in and out for an agile man of some thinness. Hardwick is thin. The disappearing act isn't so difficult if you can come and go between different rooms just by loosening a grille . . . Who else was in it?'

'The village doctor. He made chemicals for them. Hardwick could get at commercial spy apparatus. The doctor adapted them chemically.'

'Somebody adapted the commercial bugging radios to unusual frequencies and fitted out the fisherman and kept him serviced,' Marsh said. 'My guess would be either Bonus or Jass. Probably Jass, for Bonus seemed genuinely worried by the night intruder.'

'Jass,' Clarice said. 'It was hard to get him, but we paid well and persuaded him the thing was really an elaborate practical joke. Once we'd got him to start he couldn't back out.'

'Who was going to take over Mannfred's?'

'We had formed a company. Nominal capital. We could easily have got one of the big distillers interested and sold to them through our company.'

'And cleaned up handsomely,' Marsh said. 'The trouble was your husband got too impatient, too theatrical. He went too far with his fear making tricks.'

'He had to move fast once Richard went to you,' she said, bitterly.

'On the night my garage caught fire,' Marsh said, 'Hardwick was inside the building, your husband outside. When the girls ran out into the road Hardwick had only just reached his car. He feared they would suspect him and put on a show of chasing your husband in the other car to prove his own innocence.'

'Yes. They told me what had happened. But this woman was there, too. Lights out. They didn't see her car until almost too late. My husband immobilised it.'

Marsh turned to Maureen.

'Where did you go after you'd parked the car and turned the lights off?'

'I walked down the lane there to see what sort of place my husband had gone to. I was jealous. I wanted to know if there were any women there.'

Marsh went to the window and out on to the terrace. Once again he looked up at the many windows of the house. Somewhere behind one, Mary and Jane were being held. His natural impatience to find them was tempered by the thought that the longer he waited, the more relaxed the guards would become.

At the moment, there was nothing to make the Fear Makers think that any alarm had been sent out from the girls, unless the transmitter in the cigarette lighter had been spotted. Even so, they would not know the locator was in the truck, or that the signal had been picked up during the very short time it had radiated.

He went back into the room.

'Aren't you going to call the police?' Clarice said, with a return of defiance.

'With every phone in the house tapped?' Marsh said ironically. 'I think not. I want my assistants first. Where do you think they might be?'

'I don't know. That's the truth.'

'Your husband must have been using a room here.'

She sank into the chair.

'Look, I must warn you about him,' she said quickly. 'He has a wild temper. If he doesn't get his own way he'll do damage. There was a lot of money involved in this. He had been working on it for years. If he sees it being snatched away now — I think he would — do anything!'

'He must have gone off his head to have taken the girls,' Sheila said.

'He overdoes things now. That Trampleasure business. He bribed the staff to say they were people of that name,' Clarice spoke quickly, breathlessly. 'I knew he was under a strain then. He gets flamboyant. He doesn't care. He's all actor and he thinks he won't have to pay for any extravagance, as if some curtain will come down and leave him as he was before. Don't risk anything with him now. Don't risk it! I warn you!'

Marsh hesitated.

'Where's Hardwick?' he said.

'Here — somewhere. There was the photographing of the house. Good cover for him. Let him come in and out when he liked. I wish I had never — ' She broke down then and started to cry very softly. 'Don't risk anything with Gaunt. Please don't risk anything!'

Marsh waited a moment.

'Has the order gone through for the agreement to a takeover?' he said.

She looked at him with tear-filled eyes and shook her head.

'It was there, ready. It had to be signed.'

'That was what you were doing this morning in Mannfred's office?'

'Yes.'

'Your husband had been working on this for years?'

'Yes. A long time.'

'Was he a relative?'

She hesitated. 'Illegitimate. Yes. He has no claim after Richard married. Very little before, but he could just have made something from it. He resented Richard. You'll understand that.'

'When was this relationship found?'

'My husband found out accidentally. Richard didn't know until — '

'Yesterday? Today?'

'Today.'

'Where is Betsy's body?'

'I don't know. That's the truth. He says it will never be found now. He seems very sure.'

'Who set the barge off? Jass?'

'Obviously. He must have been frightened and meant to sink that dummy and drown his handiwork. He was ashamed all through of what he did for us. It was only that he used to have a hobby of wireless, building sets and things, so that he was quite handy when told what to do. There was a lot of time at night, and in the day.'

'Which was the room your husband used?'

'The east wing — ' The change had been too swift for her. She stayed with her mouth open, then closed it and dabbed the tears from her face.

Marsh went to the door.

'Keep Mrs. Gaunt company, please, Mrs. Mannfred.'

Maureen nodded. Marsh went out with Sheila close to him. 'Couldn't we get some of the staff here to help?' Sheila said uneasily.

'In the circumstances it wouldn't be wise. They don't know us well enough.'

Sheila shrugged more uneasily still.

⋆ ⋆ ⋆

Marsh went up the broad stairs to the first floor. Sheila came after him. They turned right towards the east end of the house. From its appearance it did not seem to be so much used as the other parts Marsh had seen. The doors to the rooms were often open, and either unfurnished or only very sparsely fitted out.

There was a large room at the end of the corridor, fitted out with a large, long polished table, some mahogany chairs round the walls, and on the walls crossed spears, swords, cutlasses, ritual masks and tribal shields.

'Someone of the family must have travelled and the rest don't care,' Marsh said.

She grabbed his arm suddenly. He

turned his head, and saw someone standing close to the wall alongside the door, about twelve feet away.

It was Mannfred. He began to smile as Marsh saw him, then moved slightly from the wall. He turned, very quickly and wrenched a thin sword from a pair of crossed weapons. The twin was lifted from the wall bracket and began to slither down to the floor.

'He's mad!' Sheila cried out. 'Don't — '

Mannfred lunged at Marsh's chest with the sword. Marsh grabbed a chair and swung it up. The sword was deflected off the chair and Mannfred backed, watching for another opportunity.

Marsh bent and caught the falling twin sword before it reached the floor. He dropped the chair.

'Johnny! No! He's too good, you can't — '

Sheila remembered the shattering expertness of Mannfred's fencing in the gym and she knew that John Marsh was nowhere near that standard. And these were not buttoned foils but swords meant to pierce and rip out a man's entrails.

She looked round desperately for some weapon that she might hit Mannfred with.

The swords clashed once, twice, then almost rattled with the speed of the thrust and parry. But then to her amazement, she saw Mannfred driven back.

The fat man's sword was slowing. Twice Marsh got his point to the fat belly, and then suddenly he flicked the sword from Mannfred's hand.

For a moment it seemed everyone in the room stood still, then Marsh drew back and plunged his sword into the fat paunch. Sheila shrieked. Mannfred gasped and fell back, the sword, released now, wobbled from the sagging gut.

Mannfred fell back, gasping, against the wall.

'Nearly good enough for Hamlet,' Marsh said. 'Nowhere near good enough for Mannfred!' He grabbed the sword hilt and pulled it out of the paunch. 'Where are the girls? Now, or I'll push this through your throat!'

Mannfred swallowed as the sword point

tickled his apple.

'Through the door there,' he gasped, and nodded to a door at the far end of the room.

Marsh dropped the sword, reached out, pulled the man suddenly towards him and chopped him as he went by. The man went down on his face and rolled over. Marsh put a foot on the shaggy grey hair. The wig came off.

'It looks like Hamlet!' Sheila said.

'So it is,' Marsh said.

'But his tummy — you put the sword right in — Oh, it was awful! Why isn't he bleeding?'

Marsh bent and pulled the padding cushion out of the man's big trousers. There was a hefty gash in it.

'Cheek pads and this — the likeness of a relative, the actor's ability to imitate mannerisms, the keeping his back on his 'wife' and constantly looking worriedly at the floor while talking to us this morning so we saw little of his eyes. All these things are part of the art and the act.'

He crept slowly along as he whispered, going towards the end of the room.

Nobody had shown up. Nobody seemed to have heard the clash of steel or the heavy man falling.

Marsh pushed Sheila out of the range of the door then crept up on it from the handle side. Obviously, he reckoned, someone must have heard the din of the fight, yet they were lying low behind the door.

From the layout of the other rooms leading to the end of this wing, the room beyond the main one could have no other outlet but a window thirty feet from the ground and anyone escaping would be in view of the office staff working underneath.

Marsh listened, but heard nothing.

He went back, signalled to Sheila for absolute silence, and picked up the sword.

'Just stay there with your back turned. This is a loaded gun!'

The voice from the doorway was sharp and sudden. Marsh stood there, his back towards it.

'Mary, darling, don't you recognise my back when you see it? Don't let your flaming temper do anything rash. I'm not unpuncturable.'

'Great heavens — Mary!' Sheila cried out and darted into the view of the girl at the door. 'Put the gun down!'

Mary stepped out and let the pistol fall to her side. Jane Shore appeared behind her.

'And where did you get the gun, dearest?' Marsh said, grinning as he went towards them.

'It was presented on a plate to Mr. Mannfred-Trampleasure-Gaunt,' said Jane, and pointed. 'That one down there.'

'I was imagining you a couple of helpless hostages,' Marsh said, wiping his face with a handkerchief.

'Indeed we were. That was the notion,' Mary said. 'Gaunt meant to return us only if you called off this search into Royal G.'

'Gaunt gave the gun to Hardwick to keep us quiet with,' Jane added. 'But we used one of his own tricks on him. Mary flicked her hand that way and I flicked mine this way and got him right in the Adam's apple. It was a bit of a lunge from where I was. I shall indent for a split shirt.'

'And where is Hardwick now?' Sheila asked.

'He's done his final disappearing trick,' Mary said. 'Come see.'

They went into the small room. It was just a room for lumber and stuff which had not gone into the decoration of the main room. But on the floor there was a wriggling bundle tied up in a Union Jack, the flag of the House of Royal G and an African blanket. Nothing of Hardwick was visible at all.

'Poor fellow,' said Marsh. 'Such hot weather, too. I think we'll do the same for Gaunt and then search for Mannfred.'

* * *

Mannfred was found in a boxroom in the roof, drugged and fast asleep. Sheila rang for a doctor, but not Bronson.

'Bronson was the man in the pub with Clarice,' Mary said.

'So that makes the three of them, and Hardwick four,' Marsh said. 'That's what

Clarice said. What about the waiter and the barmaid?'

'They were just fooled into thinking it was a hoax. They even laughed when Mannfred drove us out of the place in front of the gun. They thought it was a stage prop. As we went out I heard the waiter shout, 'Trampleasure!' and roar with laughter.' Jane wrinkled her nose.

'I think,' said Mary thoughtfully, 'Gaunt might have got away with this if he hadn't been so theatrical. He did do a marvellous imitation of Mannfred.'

'Big, fat, shaggy-haired cheerful men are not hard to imitate, given the start of a facial resemblance,' Marsh said. 'My guess is that he had to make up hardly at all, just fill out with pads. The time when he was most likely *not* looking like himself was when he came to LOHM.'

'I hadn't thought of it that way round,' said Sheila, frowning. 'In fact what with that and Hardwick, I seem to have picked the dud boy-friends all through this week.'

'What gave you the idea he was doubling on Mannfred?' Jane asked.

'The murder,' Marsh said. 'Both women saw him playing around with Betsy and each one thought it was her husband. Only Clarice *knew* it was hers. Maureen didn't. What had to be decided was how two different women could think their husbands were the same man. As they couldn't be the same man, they had to look like the same man. It's *Euclid*, really.'

THE END

We do hope that you have enjoyed reading this large print book.

Did you know that all of our titles are available for purchase?

We publish a wide range of high quality large print books including:
Romances, Mysteries, Classics
General Fiction
Non Fiction and Westerns

Special interest titles available in large print are:
The Little Oxford Dictionary
Music Book, Song Book
Hymn Book, Service Book

Also available from us courtesy of Oxford University Press:
Young Readers' Dictionary
(large print edition)
Young Readers' Thesaurus
(large print edition)

For further information or a free brochure, please contact us at:
Ulverscroft Large Print Books Ltd.,
The Green, Bradgate Road, Anstey,
Leicester, LE7 7FU, England.
Tel: (00 44) **0116 236 4325**
Fax: (00 44) **0116 234 0205**

Other titles in the
Linford Mystery Library:

THAT INFERNAL TRIANGLE

Mark Ashton

An aeroplane goes down in the notorious Bermuda Triangle and on board is an Englishman recently heavily insured. The suspicious insurance company calls in Dan Felsen, former RAF pilot turned private investigator. Dan soon runs into trouble, which makes him suspect the infernal triangle is being used as a front for a much more sinister reason for the disappearance. His search for clues leads him to the Bahamas, the Caribbean and into a hurricane before he resolves the mystery.

THE GUILTY WITNESSES

John Newton Chance

Jonathan Blake had become involved in finding out just who had stolen a precious statuette. A gang of amateurs had so clever a plot that they had attracted the attention of a group of international spies, who habitually used amateurs as guide dogs to secret places of treasure and other things. Then, of course, the amateurs were disposed of. Jonathan Blake found himself being shot at because the guide dogs had lost their way . . .

THIS SIDE OF HELL

Robert Charles

Corporal David Canning buried his best friend below the burning African sand. Then he was alone, with a bullet-sprayed ambulance containing five seriously injured men and one hysterical nurse in his care. He faced heat, dust, thirst and hunger; and somewhere in the area roamed almost two hundred blood-crazed tribesmen led by a white mercenary with his own desperate reasons for catching up with the sole survivors of the massacre. But Canning vowed that he would win through to safety.